Re

A REBELLIOUS HEART

Recent Titles by Margaret Pemberton from Severn House

A DARK ENCHANTMENT
FORGET-ME-NOT-BRIDE
FROM CHINA WITH LOVE
THE GIRL WHO KNEW TOO MUCH
THE LAST LETTER
MOONFLOWER MADNESS
TAPESTRY OF FEAR
UNDYING LOVE
VILLA D'ESTE
A YEAR TO ETERNITY
THE YORKSHIRE ROSE

A REBELLIOUS HEART

Margaret Pemberton

This title firs
SEVERN HC
9–15 High St
Originally pu
in 1983 by M
This title first
SEVERN HC
595 Madison

Copyright ©

To my eldest daughter,
Amanda Elizabeth,
With love.

British Library Cataloguing in Publication Data

Pemberton, Margaret
    A rebellious heart
    1. Love stories
    I.   Title
    823.9'14 [F]

    ISBN 0-7278-5809-2

Except where actual historical events and characters are being described for the storyline of this novel, all situations in this publication are fictitious and any resemblance to living persons is purely coincidental.

Printed and bound in Great Britain by
MPG Books Ltd., Bodmin, Cornwall.

CHAPTER
ONE

THE two girls strolled through the immaculately kept gardens of Lord and Lady Davencourt's town house. It was early February and though a few snowdrops braved the crisp, cold air, the carefully tended lawns were silvered with frost. The girls dug their hands deep into the warmth of their fur muffs, their ankle-length coats skimming the damp grass as they headed towards the terrace and the impatiently waiting figure of a child.

'Do hurry,' Rebecca Oversley said, stamping small, booted feet impatiently, 'I'm freezing, and Miss Cartwright is being mean and won't let me play with the dogs.'

Caroline Oversley sighed. At nineteen she had little patience with her younger sister. 'Please go inside, Becky. You'll catch a chill out here.'

With bad grace, Rebecca flounced from the terrace.

Caroline watched until she had disappeared through the French windows and into the warmth of the drawing-room before saying, 'Wretched child. Everything I say she repeats to Mama.'

Catherine Davencourt was sympathetic. Mrs Oversley had a lot in common with Lady Davencourt. Both were domineering and intolerant and petty tyrants where their children were concerned. She felt a wave of relief at the thought that soon she would no longer be answerable to her step-mother for her every action. In three weeks' time she would be Robert's wife. A warm glow suffused her slender body. Robert, Marquis of Clare: the dearest, kindest person she had ever met. She loved him with all her heart.

'Miss Cartwright leaves for Russia in two weeks,' Caroline said as they reached the foot of the terrace steps. 'Mama thinks she is too lenient and that Becky needs a stricter governess.'

Catherine's eyes widened. 'But Becky is devoted to Miss Cartwright.'

Caroline withdrew a gloved hand from her muff and traced a pattern in the light scattering of snow that lay on an ornamental stone jardinière.

'That makes no difference to Mama. She regards Miss Cartwright as too young and has engaged a veritable ogre to keep poor Becky in check. Thank goodness I am at least free from governesses.' She sighed. 'Poor Miss Cartwright. I'm sure she hasn't the slightest desire to go to Russia, but when Mama heard that Countess Vishnetskaya was looking for an English governess, she immediately suggested her.'

'But Miss Cartwright is so quiet: positively shy. I can't imagine that she would dare go all that way by herself,' Catherine protested.

'She hasn't much choice,' Caroline said practically. 'The salary Countess Vishnetskaya is paying her is far higher than any she could hope to earn in England.'

Catherine was intrigued. 'Russia,' she repeated wonderingly. 'I've never even *met* anyone who has been there. Aren't there bears, and wolves, and forests that stretch for thousands of miles?'

'I've no idea,' Caroline replied, brushing the snow from the tips of her gloves, and changing the subject to one of more interest. 'Will Dominic be attending the wedding?'

An unhappy frown puckered Catherine's brow. 'No. The Duke will not allow it.'

'His own son? But that's ridiculous. Does he mean never to see him again?'

Catherine nodded. 'Robert has tried to make him change his mind, but he says Dominic disgraced the family and he won't hear of him returning.'

'What nonsense,' Caroline said spiritedly. 'It would take more than an outraged husband to disgrace the Harlands. Dominic was only twenty, after all. It was a case of wild oats and nothing more. Someone ought to tell your future father-in-law that it's 1914, and not the middle ages.'

'The outraged husband did try to kill Dominic,' Catherine said, glancing over her shoulder to make sure there was no one within earshot. 'It wasn't just a case of harsh words.'

'The man was an exhibitionist. Fancy choosing Ascot to make a display of himself like that. I always thought Dominic behaved with great courage in disarming him. It can't be much joy facing a lunatic with a gun, especially so near the Royal Box . . .' She giggled. 'I wish I'd been there. It must have been enormous fun.'

'Not if the gun had gone off,' Catherine said chidingly to her empty-headed friend.

'Not then,' Caroline conceded. 'But as it didn't, I really can't see why he had to leave the country. Has

Robert asked that Dominic be allowed to return?'

'Yes, but it's no use. His father is quite adamant. He says that from now on he has only one son.' She paused. The Duke had forbidden Dominic's name to be mentioned, and consequently she knew very little of the man she would soon be related to by marriage. 'Have you ever met Dominic, Caroline?' she asked curiously.

Caroline raised sleek eyebrows in surprise. 'Of course. Haven't you?'

'No. I was only fourteen when it happened and he's lived on the Continent ever since. I believe he's in Paris now. I've often wondered what he's like. Mama says that he is a dissolute womaniser and that I'm not to mention his name.'

'Dominic Harland was the handsomest man in London,' Caroline said, her violet-blue eyes taking on a dreamy expression. 'He was so tall and dark. Not a bit like his father or Robert. His manners were perfect, yet underneath you felt that he didn't care about anyone or anything. That if he had wanted you he would have . . .' She gave a delicious shiver.

'Would have what?' Catherine asked innocently.

The glazed look faded from Caroline's eyes and she laughed, patting her friend affectionately on the cheek. 'When you say things like that, my pet, then I really *do* know I'm two years older than you.' She shivered again, despite the fur shoulder cape that surmounted her coat. 'So, there will be no Dominic at the wedding?'

'No. You'll have to content yourself with Bertie Pollingham.'

'Nobody could content themselves with Bertie,' Caroline said feelingly. 'He hasn't a chin.' She sighed. Without Dominic the wedding was going to be tediously dull. The Duchess was sweet but pious; the Duke was a pompous bore. As for Catherine's parents . . . Caroline suppressed a shudder. It was her opinion that Catherine would have found herself marrying Robert whether she had wanted to or not. It was no secret that death duties had financially crippled Lord Davencourt and Robert was heir to one of the richest dukedoms in England. The bride's mother would certainly shed no tears on the great day. She began to walk across the terrace towards the French windows.

'I must be going, Catherine. The Clarendons are coming for lunch.'

They stepped into the warmth of the drawing-room and immediately Rebecca leapt to her feet. 'At last! You've been simply *ages*, Caro. I thought you were never coming.'

Behind Rebecca a slim, dark-haired girl rose to her feet.

'Caroline tells me you are going to Russia in a few weeks' time,' Catherine said as Eleanor Cartwright acknowledged her presence.

'Yes, your ladyship.'

'I quite envy you. Think of all the exciting things you'll see. Cossacks, and gypsies, and horse-drawn sleighs.'

Eleanor Cartwright forced a smile. She had no desire to see any of the things Catherine had mentioned. Hers was not an adventurous spirit.

'I'm sure I shall find it all most interesting, your ladyship,' she said politely.

Rebecca pulled impatiently at her sleeve. Caroline kissed Catherine affectionately on the cheek. A footman opened exquisitely carved doors and Catherine's guests departed.

A maid relieved her of her coat, removed her boots and slid soft kid shoes on to her chilled feet.

Catherine sat reflectively by the fire, her mind once more on Robert. They were going to be happy together: joyously, deliriously happy. A soft smile curved her lips as she contemplated the idyllic future that stretched before her. It vanished abruptly as her step-mother entered the room, saying tartly,

'Has Caroline Oversley gone?'

'Yes, Mama.'

Lady Davencourt's lips tightened. Catherine's manner towards her was always beyond reproach, yet beneath the unfailing politeness, Lady Davencourt knew that Catherine disliked her—as she disliked Catherine. She disliked her startling green eyes with their long, lustrous lashes: she disliked the thick, titian hair that glinted gold beneath the light of the chandeliers and turned heads in the most crowded of rooms: she disliked her most of all because she was a living reminder of the first Lady Davencourt—a French-born beauty who still held pride of place in her husband's heart.

'I hope when you become Duchess that you will do something about the heating at Geddings. I nearly froze at dinner last night.'

'I shan't be Duchess for years, Mama,' Catherine said coolly.

'Nonsense. The Duke is ill. Everyone knows it's only a matter of time. I shall be surprised if he survives the wedding,' her step-mother said callously.

'You sound as if you want him to die.'

'Of course I don't,' Lady Davencourt lied. 'But one must face facts. Geddings is in need of a woman's touch. Robert's mother is far too wrapped up in her charities to be aware of her surroundings. And it isn't only Geddings. There's the Irish estate. I shudder to think what the furnishings are like there. The London house is passable, but that's only because Robert spends so much time in it. And the villa in Italy will need a complete overhaul.'

Catherine, who had heard it all before, excused herself and slipped quietly from the room. Her stepmother's voice floated after her. 'As for the kitchens: they'll need completely modernising . . .'

She ran up the balustraded staircase and closed her bedroom door with a sigh of relief. She sank down on the bed, folding her arms behind her head. On the dressing-table Robert's photograph smiled at her, and on the wall behind hung a full-length portrait of her grandmother. The artist had depicted her as the Goddess Diana, clothing her in a wisp of chiffon and a tantalising smile. The likeness was unmistakable. Catherine had inherited the same full-blown beauty that had made Gianetta Dubois the rage of London in the eighteen-sixties and a favourite of the Prince of Wales. Even when he had become king, Gianetta had remained a favourite, her gay wit and high spirits a constant amusement to him. And Edward VII liked to be amused.

Gianetta did not amuse her son-in-law's second wife. On the rare occasions when the latter had been included in the same house party as the King, his eyes slid over her as if she were non-existent although she could trace her lineage back to the Conqueror himself. When first her husband and then the King had died, Gianetta had retired to Paris and no one had been happier to see her go than Lady Davencourt. Even at that distance Gianetta managed to haunt her. Catherine's wedding was one instance. Gianetta would not be able to attend, owing to a riding accident.

'A *riding* accident!' Lady Davencourt had shrieked. 'A *riding* accident! Good God, the woman is seventy if she's a day!'

With his usual cowardice her husband had refrained from telling her that Gianetta's companion had been a young man of excessive good looks, somewhere in his middle twenties. What Gianetta did was her own affair, as long as she did it at a suitable distance from his wife. Lord Davencourt shared none of Gianetta's zest for life. He liked a quiet existence. A thing his present marriage made well nigh impossible.

Robert had promised her a long visit to her grandmother after their Italian honeymoon. Catherine's smile of happiness deepened. She rose from the bed and opened the drawer which held her gossamer-light négligée and silken lingerie. She was going to make Robert happy: happier than even he anticipated.

Two days later, as her landau joined in a procession through the park, Catherine caught a glimpse of Eleanor Cartwright sitting on one of the park benches. Her hand was raised to her face and it looked to Catherine as if she was crying.

'Stop, Ben!' she called to the coachman who had been in the Davencourt employ for generations.

'Hold ee on, Miss.'

The two horses immediately behind them reared up and there was the sound of feminine squeals. Catherine did not wait to apologise. She jumped from the still-rocking landau and weaved her way through the mass of strolling couples to where Eleanor Cartwright sat, her eyes overly bright, a crumpled handkerchief in her hand.

'Miss Cartwright. Can I help you? You seem distressed.'

Eleanor raised a startled face. 'It's nothing, your ladyship, just a slight cold.' She smiled bravely, but the corners of her mouth trembled.

Catherine sat down beside her. 'I don't think I believe you, Miss Cartwright,' she said gently. 'You're crying.'

A tear slid down Eleanor Cartwright's pale face as she shook her head in denial.

Catherine regarded the governess with concerned eyes. She had always liked the quiet, rather shy girl who had been engaged only a few short months ago by Mrs Oversley. It had never occurred to her to wonder if she was happy in the Oversley household. Now she was to go to Russia and all because Mrs Oversley no longer required her services. Catherine shivered in the cold, clear air. To her, Russia was a land of fairytale and romance. Perhaps it held no such magic for Eleanor Cartwright.

'Are you crying because you are leaving the Oversleys?' she asked kindly.

Eleanor took a steadying breath. 'It would be wrong of me to burden you with my troubles, your ladyship.'

Catherine covered the governess's gloved hand with her own. 'Nonsense. I wish to know. Are you unhappy at the thought of travelling to Russia?'

Eleanor Cartwright turned her head, the misery in her eyes her answer.

'There is no need for you to go,' Catherine protested. 'You could easily obtain another post in London.'

Eleanor shook her head, saying quietly, 'Mrs Oversley herself arranged my appointment with Countess Vishnetskaya. The Countess is English born and a friend of Mrs Oversley's.'

'You must tell Mrs Oversley you have no desire to take up a post so far away from England,' Catherine said firmly.

Eleanor Cartwright gave a small smile. She liked Catherine but knew she would never be able to understand the difficulties a girl in her own position faced.

'I have already done that, your ladyship.'

'Then your troubles are behind you,' Catherine said with a comforting smile.

Eleanor shook her dark head with its neat bun of plaited hair. 'Mrs Oversley was exceedingly angry at my ingratitude. She refuses to give me a reference so that I may be able to obtain another post, and truth to tell, I have no desire to do so.' She hesitated, and a faint flush mounted her cheeks. 'I . . . I intend to marry.'

Catherine gasped and then clapped her hands in delight. 'But that is marvellous news, Miss Cartwright. Who is he? And why have we not heard of him before?'

Eleanor gave a tremulous laugh. 'It is not the sort of information that Mrs Oversley would have appreciated me imparting to her children.'

'Well, you can impart it to me,' Catherine said roundly, perceiving for the first time how difficult life as a governess must be if it held so many petty restrictions.

'It is a gentleman I have known for many years. A clergyman . . .'

'And do you love him?' Catherine asked directly.

The blush on the pale cheeks deepened. 'With all my heart.'

'Then you should be radiantly happy and not indulging in tears,' Catherine chided.

The glow in Eleanor Cartwright's eyes died. 'I *am* happy. Only Algernon does not receive his curacy for another month and . . .'

'A month is nothing,' Catherine said. 'Now dry your eyes and ride with me a little and tell me where you will live and how you both met and . . .' She faltered, seeing for the first time the carpet bag at Eleanor's feet. 'Why ever are you carrying that with you in the park? It looks most cumbersome.'

Eleanor Cartwright looked as if she wished the ground would open and swallow her. Catherine continued to stare: first at Eleanor and then at the bulging bag at her feet. Slowly comprehension dawned.

'Has Mrs Oversley asked you to leave?' she asked incredulously. 'Now? Before you can marry?'

Eleanor Cartwright's agonised silence was her answer. Catherine's eyes flashed with anger.

'Come with me, Miss Cartwright,' she said decisively.

'I'm afraid I don't understand . . .'

'Come with me,' Catherine repeated and as Eleanor seemed unable to move, she picked up the bag and led the way to the waiting carriage.

'It's no use taking me back, your ladyship. Mrs Oversley was exceedingly angry.'

'I'm not taking you back, Miss Cartwright. I'm taking you home.'

'But Lady Catherine!'

Catherine ignored her protests. 'Ben, help Miss Cartwright into the carriage.'

Ben, who had been listening with interest, obeyed.

'Straight home, Ben, if you please.'

Ben picked up the reins, smiling inwardly. Her ladyship was a one and no mistake. He wondered what Lady Davencourt would say when they arrived.

'I don't understand,' Eleanor Cartwright said bewilderedly.

'It's perfectly simple, Miss Cartwright. I'm getting married in three weeks' time and until then you will act as my companion.'

'But won't Lady Davencourt object to such an unusual arrangement?' Eleanor protested.

'Undoubtedly, but Papa will not.'

To Catherine's surprise her step-mother acquiesced quite civilly to the request that Eleanor Cartwright be engaged as her companion. The wedding had caused extra work and Eleanor Cartwright was personable and well bred. She would be an asset in the flurry of the next few weeks.

That evening Eleanor sent for the remainder of her belongings. Lady Davencourt sat down to review the guest list. Catherine had the final fitting of her wedding dress. And Robert, Marquis of Clare, was brutally robbed and murdered in a London square.

It was her step-mother's piercing scream that jerked Catherine upright in her bed. For a second she thought it had been a dream, and then it came again, a scream of such anguish that Catherine leapt from her bed and fled along the darkened corridor to her step-mother's room. The lights were blazing, the bed empty. Terrified, Catherine raced downstairs, hurtling into the drawing room just in time to see one of the Duke's ashen-faced footmen leaving.

'*Oh my God! It can't be true! Frederick! Frederick!*'

Her husband tried to break her hold from the mantle-piece and failed. His wife was as cold and immovable as the marble itself. Catherine seized his arm.

'What is it, Papa? What has happened?'

Lord Davencourt gazed at his daughter awkwardly. Damn it all, it was his wife who should be telling her, not him.

'Shocking news, m'dear. Tragic.'

Icy fingers closed round her heart. 'Is it Robert?' she asked fearfully.

He cleared his throat uncomfortably. 'Dead, m'dear. Robbed and murdered. Found him not an hour ago.'

She stared at him, not hearing his clumsy words of comfort. Robert dead. Robert, with his slow smile and gentle eyes. Robert, who loved and teased her. Robert, whose calm good sense she so relied upon. That she would never feel his arms around her again seemed a thing too monstrous to be true.

'Have a brandy,' her father said inadequately, wishing she would cry, scream, anything but stare at him with that ghastly expression on her face.

She brushed the glass away, walking unseeingly back to her room. Her wedding dress hung in splendid mockery in the wardrobe. Robert's photograph smiled at her as it had always done. Outwardly everything was the same, yet in that moment Catherine knew the whole course of her life had changed. Tenderly she lifted Robert's photograph from the dressing table, holding it close to her heart, drowning it in a sea of tears.

It was two days before she emerged. Pale and hollow-eyed, and silent.

Lady Davencourt's grief was of a quite different nature.

'The fool! To *walk* home at that time of night!'

Clenching and unclenching her fists, she strode up and down the room. 'And now what? What happens to Catherine? What happens to *us*?'

'Damn it all, he didn't get murdered on purpose,' her husband said bad-temperedly, casting anxious eyes towards his daughter's room. 'Have a little charity . . .'

'Charity!' his wife screamed. '*Charity*! That's just what we'll be needing now that fool's got himself murdered!' and she continued her ceaseless marching, her fist pounding into the palm of one hand as she tried to think her way out of the impasse Robert's death had brought. Not once did it occur to her to go upstairs and comfort her bereaved step-daughter.

A week after Robert's funeral the Duke's limousine purred to a soft halt outside Lord Davencourt's London home. Catherine viewed the arrival from her bedroom window with mild curiosity. The Duke and Duchess, heavily swathed in black, disappeared from view as the butler opened the door. She looked at the clock. It was after ten. Tentatively she wondered if she should go downstairs and then decided against it. If her presence was wanted, her father would send for her.

There was no tap on her door, no summons to go downstairs, and she changed into her nightdress, brushing her hair, watching the hands of the clock move from eleven to twelve. Then, finally, there came the quiet closing of doors.

Seconds later Lady Davencourt entered her bedroom, her eyes alight with suppressed excitement.

'Catherine, I want you to listen to me most carefully. I have the most *wonderful* news.'

She sat on the bed, taking Catherine's hand in a maternal gesture, seldom used.

'The Duke and Duchess have called. There has been a complete reconciliation between Dominic and his father. The Duke has insisted that Dominic change his way of life, and that when the period of mourning is over, he marries.'

'How nice for Dominic,' Catherine said uninterestedly. 'I don't envy the girl being married solely to give Dominic respectability.'

She was glad for the Duchess's sake that the Duke had finally relented and that Dominic was once more to be welcomed at Geddings, but she couldn't share her stepmother's apparent joy at the news. After all, it was only due to Robert's death that the reconciliation was taking place.

Lady Davencourt drew a deep, trembling breath. 'Catherine! Imagine his parents' joy when he said he was prepared to marry you! That for Robert's sake . . .'

'Marry me?' Catherine stared. 'What do you mean? Marry me? Robert has only been dead a few weeks and I've never even *met* Dominic.' For the first time since Robert's death she gave a small laugh. 'I'm afraid you've been taken for the most awful leg-pull, Mama.'

Lady Davencourt clenched her teeth. 'I have *not* been taken for a leg-pull, Catherine. I am perfectly serious. You know how the Duchess adores you. The Duke has insisted Dominic marries if he is to return and so naturally the Duchess suggested . . .'

'Oh, I can imagine the Duchess suggesting it. But I can't imagine anyone taking her suggestion seriously.'

'*Dominic* took the suggestion seriously.'

Catherine's amusement waned.

'You can't possibly be serious? No one can imagine I would marry anybody so soon after Robert's death? And a man I've never met? It's ridiculous.'

'Please stop using that word. It is *not* ridiculous. It is a perfectly sensible solution to all our problems.'

'It's a sensible solution to Dominic's problems. Without a marriage satisfactory to his parents Dominic does not return to Geddings. What sort of a life must he have led if the Duke has to arrange a marriage for him? It could only be because no right-minded girl would marry him. He's *using* us, don't you see?'

'I see that once you are married to Dominic, we'll be secure,' Lady Davencourt said grimly. 'He will have to make *some* provision for us. He can't allow his parents-in-law to become paupers and that is just what we *will* become if you don't behave sensibly and marry him.'

Catherine snatched her hand from her step-mother's cold grasp. 'I'm not marrying him. Not for you. Not for anybody. There must be some way we can manage.'

'Not without Geddings!' Lady Davencourt hissed.

'You can't expect me to marry a man I've never met! A few weeks ago you were referring to him as a lecherous womaniser whose name I shouldn't mention! Now you want him for a son-in-law!'

Lady Davencourt was not used to exerting patience and her face was mottled with the effort. 'Circumstances have changed, Catherine. Of course you will accept. Dear God, the man is heir to half the Southern counties!'

'I don't care if he is heir to the throne of England,' Catherine said tightly. 'I am not marrying him!'

They faced each other, eyes blazing. Lady Davencourt made one last, strangled effort. 'There is a noble precedent for this sort of thing. Think of the King. He married his brother's bereaved betrothed.'

Catherine took a deep, quivering breath. 'There is nothing noble about it at all. I am not marrying Dominic Harland.'

Lady Davencourt's patience was at an end. She towered over Catherine, fists clenched, her face suffused with blood. 'For the last time, I am ordering you to marry the Duke!'

'He isn't a Duke yet.' Catherine sprang to her feet, refusing to be intimidated.

'He will be, my girl! He will be! And you will be a Duchess!'

Catherine stared at her incredulously. 'You are unbelievable. You don't care about me, or papa, or anyone. All you care about is getting your hands on Geddings.'

Lady Davencourt slapped her cheek hard. 'You listen to me, my girl. Your father is on the verge of bankruptcy. If you don't marry Dominic we'll be social outcasts. The Duchess is very fond of you. She believes that if you marry Dominic he will settle down. I don't care whether he does or not. But you're going to marry him,

Catherine. I'm not going to be reduced to penury because of your petty whims!'

'You can't force me to marry him!'

All her patent dislike of her step-daughter filled Lady Davencourt's face as she said, 'Can't I? I can make your life exceedingly unpleasant for you if you don't!' And she marched from the room, slamming the door behind her.

Catherine, one hand on her stinging cheek, hadn't the slightest doubt that she meant what she said. It was useless appealing to her father. He was no match for her step-mother. There was only one person who was—her grandmother. But Gianetta was in Paris with a broken leg. By the time she could come to Catherine's assistance it would be too late. There was only one solution and that was to go to Paris.

She would need money and the niggardly amount her step-mother allowed her would not be enough for the fare. She would have to borrow it from Caroline. There would be no chance to speak to her tomorrow. Catherine doubted if she would even be allowed out of her room until she had agreed to marry Dominic. If she was to see Caroline it would have to be tonight.

Even while she was thinking she was dressing, putting on her walking shoes and coat. Scarcely daring to breath she crept from the house and out into the gas-lit street.

As she headed across Sloane Square and into Symons Street, she was busy making plans. She would leave in the morning, before her step-mother rose. Lady Davencourt would think she was sulking. With luck on her side it might be evening before her presence was missed. Time enough to tell them where she was when she was safely under her grandmother's roof.

She turned sharp right into a narrow alleyway that cut ten minutes from her journey. Even if her father brought her back, Dominic would no longer wish to marry her. It would make him a laughing stock. She was so immersed in her thoughts she was not at first aware of the sound of footsteps behind her. When at last they permeated her consciousness she glanced nervously over her shoulder. In the thick darkness she saw a roughly dressed man rapidly gaining on her.

Remembering Robert's fate, Catherine did not hesitate. She picked up her skirts and ran. His feet thudded heavily after her. A hand grabbed at her shoulder. Sick with fear she wrenched away, but before she could recover her balance he had her by her coat, pulling her round, tugging at her purse.

Terrified that he would strike her if she continued to clutch it she thrust it into his hands, hurtling over the cobbles as he let her go and began to rifle through it. Dimly she heard it being tossed to one side. She ran faster, exerting every ounce of strength, but he was gaining on her, his breath harsh on her neck as his fingers grasped her shoulders ruthlessly. This time she swung round with a desperate cry, scratching wildly at his face.

He swore, grabbing her wrists cruelly, forcing her back against the wall, pressing the heavy weight of his body against hers.

She struggled frantically, screaming for help, twisting her head from side to side to avoid the leering mouth and foul breath. She gave one last piercing cry and then, so suddenly that she almost fell, she was free. She stumbled, gasping for breath, sobbing with relief.

A lithe figure hauled her attacker into the centre of the alley, punching him forcefully on the jaw, knocking him into the gutter. He staggered to his feet, head down, rushing at her rescuer like a maddened bull. The dark, cloaked figure stepped adroitly to one side, her attacker's own momentum sending him sprawling. Then, grasping the back of his collar, he hauled him to his feet, and with a well-placed boot on the rear, sent him reeling and cursing into the darkness. For a few seconds there was only the sound of his fading steps and then her rescuer adjusted kid gloves and turned to her.

'Are you hurt?'

'No. Thank you . . .' Her voice was unsteady, her breath coming in harsh gasps.

The moon sailed from a bank of cloud and she saw him clearly. He was young, tall and well-built, with thick black hair tumbling low over dark eyes. Deep frills of lace adorned the front of his shirt and emerged beneath the cuffs of his jacket, proclaiming him to be a gentleman. The evening cloak he was now idly adjusting was lined with a gleam of silk, but there was nothing of the dandy about his face. The nose was strong, the cheekbones high; the near-black eyes intimidating.

Catherine brushed a stray curl back into place and was aware that her hand was trembling. 'Thank you,' she said again, feeling the colour rise in her cheeks.

The expression on his face changed as his gaze travelled over her. Her hair had become unpinned in her flight and fell in wild disarray about her shoulders. Her breasts still heaved as she fought to regain control of her breathing. White teeth flashed in a sudden, devastating smile.

'You're too beautiful to be on the streets,' he said, eyeing her appreciatively. 'Change your profession before you get hurt or murdered.'

She gasped, hardly able to believe her ears.

'How dare you!' she cried, raising her hand to deliver a stinging blow to his cheek. He moved swiftly, catching her wrist in a steel-like grip, his eyes hot and dark as he bent his head, kissing her until she lost her breath in the passion of his mouth. Heat surged through her body as his lips seared hers, his body pinioning her against the cold damp of the wall.

As suddenly as he had seized her he released her, gazing down at her with a mixture of amusement and regret, chucking her under the chin with insulting intimacy, before striding off into the darkness.

As his footsteps faded, Catherine remained against the wall, leaning on it for support, her heart beating wildly and irregularly. Slowly she raised a trembling hand to her burning lips. Only Robert had ever kissed her: and not even he had done so with such indecent thoroughness. Shame suffused her. Why, with his lips on hers, had she not struggled to be free? The answer brought the blood stinging to her cheeks. She had not struggled to be free because she had not desired to be free. With a sob she picked up her skirts and began to run in the direction of the Oversley town house.

On reaching it she rapped on the door with an unsteady hand. A frightened looking maid promised to bring Caroline down, leaving Catherine shivering in the hallway. A few minutes later Caroline was swearing the maid to secrecy and ushering a dishevelled Catherine into the drawing room.

'Whatever has happened, Catherine?' Caroline asked, her violet-blue eyes wide and shocked.

Catherine's body still felt as if it were on fire, throbbing with an emotion she was powerless to control. She said with difficulty, 'They want me to marry Dominic and I won't. I'm going to my grandmother in Paris. I haven't any money of my own, Caroline. I thought you might be able to help me.'

Caroline gazed round-eyed at the bruises on Catherine's wrists. 'Did *Dominic* do that to you?'

Catherine gazed down at the bruises and flushed.

'No. I came through the alley and a man followed me.' Her voice began to shake. 'He stole my purse and then . . .'

Caroline stared, horrified.

'He was going to . . . I feel sick, Caroline.'

Hastily Caroline poured her a brandy.

'He was touching me, pressing against me.' She shuddered. 'Someone heard me scream. He pulled the man off.'

'And?' Caroline asked, mesmerised.

'And that was all.' She fought down the memory of her rescuer. Of the feel of his body against hers. Of the claiming, unhesitant mouth. Of her shameless response.

'Are you feeling all right?' Caroline asked curiously. 'You're trembling.'

'It's nothing,' Catherine lied, the blood surging through her body in a red-hot tide. 'Can you get me the money, Caroline?'

'Yes. But you're making a big mistake, Catherine. If Dominic wants to marry you, you should leap at the chance. I would.'

'What! Marry a man so that he can return home the
prodigal son?'

Caroline shook her head. 'Dominic wouldn't marry
for convenience. He and Robert were very close and
used to meet often without their father's knowledge.
It's my guess Dominic has seen you many times with
Robert when you were in France, visiting your grandmother.'

Catherine stared at her. 'But why shouldn't Robert
have introduced us openly?'

'And risk the Duke's wrath if you should have in-
advertently let it slip? Far easier for you, my sweet, if
you knew nothing. Don't act rashly. Wait until you see
him then make your decision.'

'No.' Catherine pushed the shining mass of her hair
away from her face. 'I couldn't love anyone else as I did
Robert.'

She felt such pain at her infidelity of a few moments
ago that the breath caught in her throat and she could
hardly speak. 'Please give me the money, Caroline. My
grandmother will understand. She'll look after me.'

Caroline sighed. 'Very well. If your mind is made up.'

As she rose to her feet there came the unmistakable
sound of a fist pounding hard on the outside door.
Caroline's father hurried confusedly downstairs, fum-
bling with his dressing gown. Seconds later he was facing
a raging Lord Davencourt.

'Is my daughter here?' Lord Davencourt thundered.
'By God, Oversley, if you've encouraged her in this
foolishness I'll never forgive you!'

'What the devil do you mean?' Caroline's father asked
bewilderedly. 'What *is* this? Stop waving your cane at

me in that stupid manner, Davencourt. It's the middle of the night.'

'I'm well aware what time it is!' Lord Davencourt brushed past Mr Oversley and pushed open the drawing-room door.

The two girls clutched at each other as their fathers' wrath exploded round them.

'*Home!*' Lord Davencourt bellowed.

'*To bed!*' Caroline's father commanded, red with rage at the disturbance of his sleep and fearful of what scrape his empty-headed daughter had got herself into.

'It isn't Caroline's fault. She didn't know I was coming. I . . .'

'*Home!*' Lord Davencourt frothed at the mouth.

'Some explanation, old man,' Mr Oversley said, relieved that Davencourt's wrath was centred entirely on Catherine.

'Family matter.' Lord Davencourt said, pushing rudely past him as he dragged his unwilling daughter in his wake. 'Speak to you in the morning.'

Lord Davencourt's fury was nothing to that of his wife. Even Catherine had shrunk before her stepmother's ice-cold rage. Lady Davencourt, knowing only too well that if she took a cane to Catherine she would kill her, had with enormous self-control commanded that Catherine be locked in her room and stay there until she regained her senses.

It was midday before the key turned and Eleanor entered with a tray of water and two thin slices of bread. Outside, and trying not to look uncomfortable, stood two of the footmen.

Catherine laughed mirthlessly. 'Did Mama think that

I would attack you and try to escape?'

'I don't know, Lady Catherine,' Eleanor said truthfully. 'Lady Davencourt is exceedingly angry.'

'She always is if she isn't having her own way. I wish I were you, Eleanor: marrying a man I loved – or even going to Russia.'

'I can't stay, Lady Catherine. Lady Davencourt gave me strict instructions simply to leave the tray in the room.'

Catherine's eyes sparked with an expression that would have made her step-mother instantly wary. 'Have you still got your passport and sailing ticket, Eleanor?'

'Yes . . .'

'And the Vishnetskis can't have heard yet that you're not going?'

'I wouldn't know, your ladyship.'

Catherine's eyes gleamed. 'The next time you bring my tray, bring your passport, ticket and letter of introduction to Countess Vishnetskaya, and take this money and buy me a brown hair dye.'

'Hair dye, Lady Catherine?' Eleanor asked, horrified.

'Yes. I helped you, Eleanor. Now I want you to help me. I'm going to the Vishnetskis' in your place.'

'But you can't, Lady Catherine,' Eleanor said, aghast. 'Not as a governess.'

'Caroline told me your main duties would be to teach the children French and English. My French is far better than yours. Of course I can go.'

'But Lady Catherine!' Eleanor's eyes were agonised.

'There's nothing to be afraid of. You leave here next week. No one will ever know.'

Wretchedly Eleanor left the room and Catherine sat

back on the bed, filled with determination. She would go as governess to the Vishnetskis and save her salary. When she had enough she would leave and join her grandmother in Paris. While she waited for Eleanor's return she carefully wrote a letter to the Countess. In it she explained that Mrs Oversley had been taken ill and could not write herself. That would take care of the discrepancies in handwriting. Then she wrote that any previous letter was to be ignored. Eleanor Cartwright would arrive as arranged.

That evening Eleanor brought Catherine all she had asked for and Catherine gave her the letter to post. Next day when Lady Davencourt swept into the bedroom, ready to do battle, she was pleasantly surprised at the effect two days of isolation and a diet of bread and water had had on her step-daughter. Submissively Catherine listened to her once more explain the necessity of marrying Dominic. Unwillingly, and with a tear or two, she acquiesced. Lady Davencourt breathed a heartfelt sigh of relief.

'I'm glad you have come to your senses, Catherine. The Duchess has arranged a private dinner party for us on Saturday evening. You will meet Dominic then. Everything will have to be very quiet, of course. A private ceremony. Perhaps a pearl-grey dress in the circumstances.'

The boat sailed on Friday night. Briefly Catherine agreed that pearl-grey would suit her very well. Lady Davencourt, unable to believe her good fortune, agreed.

Late on Thursday night Catherine dyed her hair, changing it from fiery red to a drab, dark brown. She drew it back, plaiting it in a bun, the way Eleanor did. The likeness was not startling, but they were both young and had the same coloured eyes, and perhaps, thought Catherine optimistically, the customs officer would have defective eyesight. She spent some time composing a goodbye note to her parents. Finally she wrote only that she was leaving home rather than marry a man she didn't love, or suffer her step-mother's rage if she didn't. Then she packed her things into Eleanor's carpet-bag, tucked her ticket down her bodice, and waited for dawn. When it came, she crept stealthily from her home. This time for good.

CHAPTER
TWO

THAT day was the longest in Catherine's life. Every foot-fall, every accidental touch of her shoulder had her jumping like a frightened rabbit. Not till the first smoky light of dusk did she begin to relax. The docks were crowded with would-be passengers and stacks of cargo. Through the noise and confusion Catherine threaded her way to the *Gretel*, the small German cargo boat that was to take Miss Eleanor Cartwright to St Petersburg. All around her fond farewells were being said, tears shed. Dry-eyed and exultant, Catherine stepped alone onto the gangplank and presented her ticket.

Her cabin was small but the porthole faced the docks. For the next couple of hours Catherine curled up on her bunk, watching the last of the cargo being loaded and last-minute passengers hurrying up the gangplank. A haze of fog was sweeping in from the sea when the horns finally blared and the sailors prepared to cast off. There was some confusion as a carriage sped to a halt, sending a pile of crates flying. A dark figure ran lightly to the dock side, taking the widening gap between quay and gangplank with an easy spring. Catherine's heart began to beat wildly. For a brief minute she had thought it was the dark-eyed stranger and then common sense asserted itself. The *Gretel* was a cargo boat; hardly the type of vessel her immaculately dressed rescuer would choose to travel in. For the hundredth time she remembered the abrasively masculine lines of his face and his kiss and wondered who he was. The fog horns blared and the cargo boat began to make its way down the Thames and into the North Sea. Whoever he was, she would never see him again.

The next morning she awoke to a violent pitching and tossing. She spent a few minutes adjusting to the motion of the boat and then dressed quickly, struggling along the swaying corridor and up on to the deck. A strong wind was blowing and above the boat gulls wheeled and screamed, diving down to scavenge whatever they could. The cold air had driven all but the hardiest passengers below. The movement of the boat had no adverse effect on Catherine. She found the vast expanse of plunging grey waves exhilarating. As she walked into the wind a fine rain blew against her face, whipping her cheeks with colour.

She ignored the admiring glances of a seaman coiling rope and continued along the deck, wondering what time breakfast would be served and if it would be palatable. As she approached the stern she stopped short. Not ten yards away from her, as impervious to the motion of the boat as herself, stood her rescuer.

Although he had his back towards her, there was no mistaking his air of easy assurance. The young man with him did not look to be enjoying his journey. His skin was pallid, his expression wretched. Her first instinct was to turn, her second to get a closer look at him. As he moved into profile and in the clear light of day, she saw that his complexion was honey-toned, almost gypsy like, and she wondered if perhaps he had Russian blood in his veins. His black hair was springy as heather, curling tightly in the nape of his neck and in the early morning sunshine he looked handsomer than ever. Her eyes were drawn to his mouth and as she remembered his kiss her face burned. He raised his head and before she could turn his eyes met hers, and his dark brows flew upwards in surprised recognition.

She turned in confusion, walking quickly away from him, but even as she did so she heard the quick tread of his feet following her, and then a hand was laid lightly on her arm, restraining her.

'We seem to meet in the most unusual circumstances.' His voice held a note of laughter that brought the colour to her cheeks.

'I would prefer to forget our first meeting, sir,' she said, struggling for composure. 'The circumstances were most unfortunate.'

This time there was no mistaking the amusement in the near black eyes.

'*Most* unfortunate,' he agreed, falling into step beside her.

The warmth of his breath stirred on her neck and a tremor ran through her body. A gentleman would apologise for his previous behaviour and put her at her ease. Her companion seemed to have no such intention.

She avoided his gaze, knowing that if she held it any longer the colour would rise beneath her skin.

'Where are you bound for?' he asked with easy familiarity.

It was obvious that no apology was to be forthcoming. Anger surged through her. His behaviour was disrespectful, insulting.

'To St Petersburg—as a governess,' she replied tartly. Being a governess was the height of respectability and her admission would certainly put him in his place. But how much better to have been able to give him a real set-down and admit to being Lady Catherine Davencourt. She raged inwardly. Her subterfuge was already having drawbacks, and of the kind she had not envisaged.

She had caught his interest. 'St Petersburg?' Winged eyebrows rose fractionally.

'Yes. I am going as governess to the children of Countess Vishnetskaya.'

He stopped short, his eyes darkening in disbelief.

'I hope you did not think I would be joining a more humble household,' Catherine said, glad that she had shaken his insufferable complacency.

'Of course not.'

There was something in his voice that made her look sharply at him. Was he laughing at her?

'It just so happens that I am acquainted with the Vishnetski family.'

'Oh!' Catherine was nonplussed.

There was unexpected kindness in his voice as he said, 'Perhaps I could tell you a little about them?'

Catherine forgot his previous insolence and said with naive eagerness, 'Oh yes. I would like that.'

He smiled down at her and the breath caught in her throat. It was hard to remain angry with him when he looked at her with such frank appraisal.

'The Countess is English, but then you will know that already?'

Catherine nodded, trying to remember frantically the sparse bits of information that Eleanor had passed on to her:

'She is a very beautiful woman and a very sweet one.'

Catherine felt a surge of relief. Of her employer's beauty she was uncaring, but a kindly disposition would be of paramount importance.

'I am sure you will enjoy the parties and balls in St Petersburg.'

Catherine looked at him quickly, sure that he was mocking her. The high-cheekboned face with the square-cut chin and well-shaped mouth betrayed nothing.

'I am going as a governess, sir. Not as a visitor,' she said frostily.

'Oh, but governesses are treated as family in Russia. It is not at all like England. It is quite common practice for governesses to attend the parties and balls given by their mistresses.'

Catherine stared at him aghast. The only dresses she had brought with her were those she had thought suitable for a governess. To have to endure parties and balls in serviceable high-necked dresses . . . The thought was appalling.

'And it wouldn't surprise me if Princess Dagmar requested your services too. Mrs Oversley told me that on her last visit she requisitioned anyone of intelligence to accompany her.'

Catherine gasped, thrown into total confusion. It had never occurred to her that she would be mixing with ladies of such high rank as princesses, and as for the stranger at her side being acquainted with Mrs Oversley . . . She grasped the deck rail for support.

'You look rather pale?' His deep-timbred voice was concerned.

Catherine looked away from him hastily, studying the heaving waves with undue concentration.

'It is nothing; the motion of the boat. Do you know Mrs Oversley well?'

'I said goodbye to her only yesterday. But if you're wanting anecdotes about the aristocracy, you are wasting your time.'

Catherine had to bite her lip to stop herself from telling him that the daughter of Lord Davencourt needed no anecdotes. And who was he anyway? Rude and condescending though he was, his face and figure were devastating. Yet Caroline had never mentioned any visitor that had made her heart beat faster. And Catherine was sure that if Caroline had met him she would have talked of nothing else for days. Before she could ask, he said drily, 'And in St Petersburg, it won't be only lords and ladies you will be mixing with. It will be princes and princesses. The Princess Dagmar lives permanently at Verechenko.'

Despite herself, Catherine's interest was caught.

'Is the Princess young?'

A slight smile tinged his mouth. 'Princess Dagmar is eighty if she's a day.'

'Oh.' Catherine was disappointed. An elderly princess was not very glamorous.

Reading her mind he said, 'But her grandson, Kiril, is young and pretty enough for the two of them.'

This time there was no mistaking the underlying
amusement in his voice. Catherine, because she did not
understand what was amusing him, ignored the remark,
refusing to show any interest in Prince Kiril. They had
reached the companionway leading down to the dining
saloon and she held her hand out stiffly to say goodbye.
He took it lightly and to her complete consternation
lifted it to his lips.

'Perhaps we will meet again, Miss . . .'

'Cartwright,' Catherine stammered as the heat of his
lips seared the back of her hand.

'I would be obliged if you would give my compliments
to the Countess.'

'But I don't know your name,' Catherine protested,
her hand still held prisoner.

'True.' His eyes held hers and she could see flecks of
gold in the dark pupils. Time wavered and halted. He
released her hand.

'Dominic Harland, Marquis of Clare,' he said.

Catherine felt as if she had been physically struck.
There was a thundering in her ears, and the face in front
of her and the deck and the sea swam in a juggling
kaleidoscope of colour and light. Tightly she held on to
the rail. The pain in her chest crushed the breath out of
her.

If he was aware of her consternation he showed no
sign of it and his next words were like a knife wound. 'I
am gratified that you took my advice, Miss Cartwright,
and changed your profession. Your present one does
you credit. You can trust that I shall not breathe a word
of your previous occupation to anybody in St Petersburg.'

Blindly Catherine turned away from him, pushing past the other passengers and hurrying into the dining saloon. How dare he speak to her in such a manner? How could fate be so cruel? Why, in a flight to escape a marriage of convenience to him, was she to be thrown into his company? And what, she thought suddenly, was he doing aboard the *Gretel* on his way to Russia, when he should have been waiting to meet her in London? The room steadied around her. She found some of the other passengers gazing at her curiously and with immense effort strove to breathe normally and appear calm. Not even her step-mother would be aware yet that she had fled. Was Dominic jilting her? It was typical of what she knew of him that he had offered to marry her and then reneged on it for the sheer amusement such an exercise would afford him. She clenched her teeth and fought back bitter tears. How could Robert, so sweet and kind, have possibly had a brother so utterly . . . utterly . . .

'Breakfast, Miss?' the steward asked.

She looked at him blankly.

'Breakfast, Miss?' he asked again, wondering how such feather-brained young women managed to hold down responsible positions in alien lands.

'Oh yes . . . Thank you.' She drank the hot, bitter coffee gratefully.

At least she had done the right thing. Left immediately, not giving him the chance to have a joke at her expense. The thought gave her some satisfaction. He had been arrogant enough to have assumed she would marry him sight unseen. No doubt he was used to young ladies vying for his favours and being grateful for any crumb of attention he should give them. Well, he had

made a mistake where Catherine Davencourt was concerned. Instead of receiving news that she had waited to
meet him and accept his proposal and been distraught at
his rejection, he would hear that she too had never
condescended to attend the dinner party their parents
had arranged. Perhaps *that* would take the smile off his
laughing face.

The steward grinned at her. She might be feather-
brained, but she was certainly a cut above the usual
young women making the crossing.

'I see the rolling of the ship doesn't upset you, Miss?'

'No.' Catherine was unaccustomed to those serving
her speaking with such familiarity. It was another thing
she would have to get used to, and his manner was
pleasant enough.

'Most of the other passengers are keeping to their
bunks till we reach the Kiel and a bit o' calm. There's
plenty of coffee if you want some more.' He winked at
her. 'You just give me the nod, Miss. I'll see you're all
right.'

Catherine ate hurriedly. It had suddenly occurred to
her that the Marquis, too, was unaffected by the motion
of the ship and would be coming into the dining saloon to
eat. She was determined to avoid another meeting whilst
they were on board. She walked quickly back to her
cabin, leaving it only for meals, until the boat entered
the smooth waters of the Kiel Canal. Then, taking care
not to walk in the direction of the stern, she stayed for
hour after hour at the deckrail, watching the flying
spumes of spray as the boat ploughed on into the icy
vastness of the Baltic and the freezing cold drove her
below decks once again.

'St Petersburg in the morning,' said the steward who had taken her under his wing. 'If you want to see it at its best, get up early, just as the sun is rising.'

'Will we be there so soon?'

'Yes. But depending on the ice it could be mid-day before we disembark. How about another cup of coffee. There's some fresh made.'

Excitement woke her with the first pale rays of dawn. Quickly she dressed and went up on deck. The sea was iced over, the cold making her gasp for breath. All around small boats rocked, futilely trapped, but the cargo boat forged slowly onwards aided by a giant ice-cutter. And ahead, breathtaking in its splendour, stood the fairytale city of St Petersburg.

Delicate spires rose ethereally in the early morning mist. Pumpkin-shaped domes glittered. Towers and steeples shimmered under a hoar of frost. Golden turrets and pinnacles pierced the sky, and from giant cupolas there came the magical tolling of bells.

Ecstatically Catherine leaned on the deckrail, the ice cracking as the *Gretel* forced its way nearer and nearer to its dreamlike destination.

Disembarking was more chaotic than embarking, and she was crushed in a rush of passengers and trunks and baggage as she struggled to make her way down the gangplank. Clutching her bag tightly she stared around her in bewilderment on the dockside.

Where should she go? What should she do? As she tried to gather her scattered wits she saw Dominic Harland disembark, his trunks carried by several of the crew, his young companion obviously grateful to feel dry land beneath his feet again. Although Dominic did not look in her direction, his companion did and their eyes met. She saw him touch Dominic's arm and speak to him. Still the Marquis's head did not turn. But his voice carried carelessly over the clamour around him.

'No one you know. Only a pretty street-walker out for better pickings on the Continent.'

If it hadn't been for the mass of people between them she would have flown at him demanding an apology. As it was they were already moving away and a stern-faced official was asking for her passport. To her relief he handed it back to her after scarcely looking at the photograph.

Above the noise of greetings and the sound of church bells there came the not too distant sound of a loud military band. Then, above the babble and confusion, Catherine heard her name being boomed out.

'Miss Cartwright! Miss Cartwright!'

A burly Russian in flowing driving cloak and knee-high boots was forcing his way through the crowd. She waved and his face lit with a yellow smile. Through a black mass of hair and beard he said in broken English, 'Miss Cartwright for Countess Vishnetskaya?'

'Yes.'

'Dmitri.' He grinned again, taking her bag.

The street was nearly as noisy and crowded as the docks and an Arctic blast seared through her thin coat. With a surge of elation she saw a sleigh waiting to take her to Verechenko. Dmitri seated her carefully, wrapping a thick rug over her knees. As he did so she saw the Marquis. No icy blasts were disturbing *him*. He now wore an ankle-length sable coat and was stepping into a luxuriously furred troika. She wrapped the rug closely round her knees, watching as the troika flashed past, bells jingling, lost immediately in the swarming streets.

The sleigh eased away from the docks, speeding over the cobbles, troikas and sledges skimming out of the way. She caught a glimpse of a gilded opera house and bazaar crammed with brilliantly coloured shawls. There were street stalls with live birds for sale and hot pies being sold at street corners. Everywhere there were soldiers in braided overcoats, flying carriages, and over and above all else, noise.

The noise of church bells, of the shouts of the coach-men, of street sellers, of pounding hooves. It was what she had hoped for and anticipated. An entirely new world. She caught a glimpse of fabulous necklaces and bracelets in a jewellers and incredibly ragged children being cuffed and pushed by the police for loitering outside the windows. A lone musician strode casually down the street, the sound of his accordion vying with that of the band and bells.

The sleigh speeded over a crowded bridge spanning the Neva, carriages and pedestrians hurrying out of the way. The early morning sun cast tongues of flame on the steel-grey water and couples sauntered hand in hand along the banks.

They crossed to the Islands and behind gigantic gates she glimpsed beautiful gardens and opulent houses and then Dmitri was turning between towering statues of lions and the noise of the city faded.

The palace glowed like a precious stone in the North-ern sunlight. The lower floor was a series of archways leading onto a marble terrace. On the balcony above, white pillars supported a gilded roof. In the gardens were fountains, icicles hanging from bronze dolphins and naiads. Doves clustered for warmth around a dove cote, cooing soothingly. The sleigh came to a halt. Dmitri helped her descend on to the tightly packed snow and as her heart hammered in nervous anticipation, a richly liveried footman opened the door and she shook out her skirts, took a deep breath, and entered the palace that was to be her future home.

CHAPTER
THREE

DOUBLE doors opened and closed endlessly as Catherine followed the footman through room after room, up a long flight of red-carpeted stairs, along a gallery lined with marble busts. Open doors patterned in gold gave a glimpse of a ballroom with huge, glittering crystal chandeliers. The rooms they passed through were crowded with small tables strewn with glass-topped collections of miniatures, enamelled scent flasks, jewelled snuff boxes. On heavier marble-topped tables were Dresden shepherdesses, Meissen and Wedgwood, ivory and jade figurines. The walls were covered with exquisite panelling, the high ceilings supported by Corinthian pillars, the furnishings all gilt and brocade. At last the footman opened double doors of delicately carved rosewood and Catherine walked nervously into a salon ablaze with light. A huge log fire leaped and flamed and beside it, her legs covered with a silver fur, a plump woman with fair hair and friendly eyes lay on a chaise longue.

'The governess, Barina,' the footman said, retreating and closing the mahogany doors behind him.

Catherine stepped forward, encouraged by the sweet expression on the smiling face.

'My dear, you look as though you have strolled

through Hyde Park, not endured a nightmare sea journey.'

'I enjoyed it,' Catherine said, knowing that she would have been speaking the truth if it hadn't been for Dominic Harland's unwelcome presence.

The countess laughed, indicating a chair with a wave of a soft hand. 'To be a good traveller is a distinct advantage in Russia. The distances are so vast it is impossible to imagine. And always it is cold.' She shivered. 'The summer is no sooner here than it is gone. What is the weather like in England now?'

'Beautiful. The almond trees are in flower and the parks are a mass of daffodils.'

'And the bluebells? Are there bluebells in the woods?'

'Yes . . .' Catherine's heart was touched by the wistfulness on the pretty face. She had no idea how to address her and ended up awkwardly as the footman had done, saying: 'Yes, Barina.'

The Countess smiled. 'You are already picking up correct expressions. Your position is higher than that of a servant. They will refer to you as Barishna. The children will speak French or English at all times and to them you will be Miss Eleanor.'

'My duties . . .' Catherine began apprehensively.

'To speak French and English to them and occupy them during the day. The Russians have very different ideas on bringing up children than we English. I did have a French governess, but she left after a few months. She was totally unable to control them. Natasha is seven and Alexander is four. All those years with a Russian nanny cannot be eradicated in only months. I am afraid you will have to be very strict with them. Olga will feel she is being usurped, but it is my wish that the children are brought up with English manners and I give you complete control over them. If I were not so handicapped,' her soft hand moved slightly to indicate her legs hidden by the fur, 'I should have been able to have influenced them myself. As it is I must rely on you, Eleanor.'

With a surge of pity Catherine realised that the semi-recumbent position was not one of grace or idleness, but one of sickness. The Countess saw the expression before she could hide it.

'I was thrown from a horse shortly after the birth of Alexander. You can imagine how much it means to me to have a fellow-countrywoman to talk to when my world is so restricted.'

'I'm sorry . . .'

'Don't be,' she said gently. 'Everything is God's will. That is what Russians believe and it helps to believe it as well. Alice, my maid, is English. She came out with me when I married. She will be pleased to have someone to talk to. She cannot speak French and in nine years has learned no Russian. She will also be an ally if Olga should prove too awkward.'

'Is Olga the children's nanny?'

'Yes. But don't let her intimidate you. I want you to be happy with us, Eleanor.'

'I will be,' Catherine said with growing confidence. 'When do I meet the children?'

'The morning will be soon enough for that ordeal,' the Countess said with a smile. 'There's a hot meal waiting for you and then you can settle yourself in your room. Goodnight, Eleanor.'

Relieved that her role was going to be so easy to play,

Catherine followed the footman back through interminable rooms, to a magnificent dining-room where she ate in solitary splendour. Then he led her upstairs. No meanly furnished room here as there had been for Eleanor Cartwright in the Oversley household.

There was pretty patterned wallpaper and lilac upholstery and a sumptuous bed draped in chiffon. A fire burned brightly, casting a rosy glow onto a sturdy desk and comfortable-looking chairs. Slim windows looked out over the moonlit grandeur of sparkling snow and the black silhouettes of pine trees. She put the few things she had brought with her into the drawers and set her brush and comb on the desk top, changing into her nightdress and snuggling down into the big bed without the least trace of homesickness. One phase of her life was over, another was about to begin.

She woke to find two laughing fiends bouncing on her bed and pounding her with pillows.

'I'm Alexander!'

'I'm Natasha!'

The pillows rained on her shoulders as she struggled to sit up.

'Stop it this minute. *Immediately!*'

'Speak French,' Natasha chanted, jumping off the bed out of reach. 'You have to speak French.'

'And you have to behave,' Catherine said, struggling into her dressing gown as Alexander did his best to pull it away from her.

'Oh, but we *always* behave, don't we, Alexander? Olga says we're perfect angels.'

'And do you behave like this with her?'

'Yes, but Olga can't catch us. She's too old and fat.'

The two children, temporarily exhausted, sat cross-legged on the floor.

'She's prettier than Mam'selle,' Natasha said to her brother, as if Catherine were non-existent.

'Pretty,' her little brother agreed.

'And she doesn't cry like Mam'selle did.'

'Doesn't cry,' Alexander agreed solemnly.

Catherine was already feeling a great deal of compassion for her predecessor. She shooed them from the room while she washed and dressed and then, as the noise from the far side of the door reached alarming proportions, she bade them enter while she finished braiding her hair and then turned to them, her hands folded in her lap, trying to look as commanding as possible.

'Mam'selle was French. *I* am English.'

The children waited expectantly, chins resting on their hands, eyes unwavering.

'English governesses do not cry. They like children who are well-behaved and polite. It was polite of you to come in and say good morning. It was *not* polite to hit me with pillows and pull my hair.'

'But it was fun,' Natasha protested.

'Fun,' the little echo by her side said.

'It was not fun for me. Now, it's a nice day and the sun is out. Perhaps you could show me around the grounds.'

'Can you skate?' Natasha asked, her eyes lighting up. 'Mam'selle wouldn't go outside because it was too cold and she said I could only skate when Papa was home. The ice on the lake will be thinning soon and then it will be too late.'

'I'll take you skating *if* you are well-mannered and polite.'

'Can't skate,' Alexander said, his chin trembling.

Catherine leaned forward and took a sturdy little hand in hers. 'Then I will teach you. Come on. You still have to dress yet.'

'We don't dress ourselves. Olga dresses us.'

'Then it's about time you did,' Catherine said spiritedly.

Alexander remained on the floor, brown eyes holding hers compellingly.

'Can't,' he said. 'Only four.'

'Then I'll help you. You'll need lots of warm things. It's very cold out.' With his hand in hers he trotted happily by her side, her first conquest in an alien land.

Olga, encased in black from head to foot, wept at the sight of Natasha pulling on her own stockings. Catherine, not wanting to cause bad feeling unnecessarily, left Alexander with her to be swamped with tears and endearments as she dressed him in a high-necked, loosely-belted silk shirt and soft trousers tucked into felt boots so that he looked exactly like the Cossacks of Catherine's imagination. When Catherine handed Olga his outdoor clothes she screamed with horror, pointing outside to the snow and clutching Alexander to her massive bosom, as if exposure to fresh air would result in the instant death of her darling. Every time Catherine approached Alexander, Olga's screams increased and soon there was a group of interested-looking servants in the doorway. Taking Natasha by the hand, Catherine marched purposefully to the salon.

The Countess laughed. 'Poor Olga. The next few

weeks are not going to be easy for either of you. Dmitri, get the children their skates and find a pair for Miss Eleanor, and bring Alexander and Olga downstairs to me.'

As they entered the salon Alexander twisted from Olga's grasp, running with a beaming smile towards Catherine. As she watched him Olga's eyes darkened with jealousy. Unknowingly Catherine had made an enemy.

'Miss Eleanor is replacing Mam'selle as governess to the children, Olga,' the Countess said pleasantly. 'That means that outside the nursery she has complete control over them.'

Olga's thin lips tightened so much they disappeared altogether.

'If Eleanor wants to take the children skating there are to be no objections. Fresh air, however cold, is more beneficial to them than staying in stuffy, over-heated rooms all day. It would do you good to take a walk yourself, Olga.'

Olga's doughy face blanched. 'She made Natasha *dress* herself, Barina,' she protested.

'Good,' the Countess said unperturbed. 'It is time that she did so.'

'But she's treating the children like peasants! Like serfs!'

'She is treating them like English children.'

'But they are *Russians*!' Olga spat defiantly.

There was a strained silence, then the Countess said quietly, 'You forget that I, too, am English. Remember to whom you are speaking, Olga Nikolaievna.'

Sullenly Olga backed away, going straight to the

kitchens where she informed the rest of the household that the Barina and the English governess were intent on killing Alexander and the sooner the Count came home the better.

The Countess turned with a smile to Catherine. 'I told you it wouldn't be easy,' she said. 'But if you continue to be pleasant despite Olga's sourness the battle will soon be won.'

Catherine sincerely hoped so. She didn't want too many repetitions of Olga's tantrums and the grinning audience of servants.

'Verechenko is relatively quiet at the moment. Alexis, my husband, returns from his estates near the Finnish border today or tomorrow. His Great-Aunt, Princess Dagmar Dolgorova, is at present holidaying in the Crimea. She spends most of the year with us here in St Petersburg and should be back by the end of the month. Don't let her intimidate you. She appears fierce but has a heart of gold. When her son and daughter-in-law were tragically drowned she took her grandson, Kiril, into her own care and is devoted to him. Prince Kiril has his own suite of rooms in the west wing. The only other resident at Verechenko is Baroness Kerenskaya, Princess Dagmar's companion. Naturally everyone speaks English so you will have no language problem, but French is the language most Russians use socially.'

'How strange.'

The Countess laughed. 'You will find a lot of things strange in St Petersburg, but you can always rely on my help and support.'

She leaned back against her cushions and Catherine sensed that she was dismissed. Taking the children by the hand she led them out into the freezing sunshine.

It was hard to believe that Verechenko was in the middle of a city. Terraces and lawns swept gently in a vista of white to a small lake half hidden amongst larch and pines. Catherine lifted Alexander high into the air to knock snow off the stone lions flanking the steps, then she tapped Natasha on the shoulder crying, 'Catch' and ran away with a giggling Alexander behind her. A squirrel darted out of the way as they chased each other, and a flock of geese rose protestingly at the unaccustomed noise, winging away to a quieter spot.

'Oh, this is *fun*,' Natasha said delightedly as she flew daringly across the ice, Catherine close behind her. They raced each other with Natasha shrieking merrily every time Catherine allowed her to win. Then Catherine showed her some new, more difficult steps, which impressed Natasha profoundly.

'Even Papa cannot skate like that. You *are* clever. Is this how you do it?' And time after time she tried, laughing whenever her feet shot out from under her. Finally, when she had mastered the new steps, she linked hands with Catherine and they glided back to the bank where Alexander waited apple-cheeked. Holding his hands Catherine led him gently out onto the ice. Radiant eyes held hers as he tottered joyfully along, faltering and falling, bringing Catherine down with him.

From the bank came loud clapping. Catherine, sat unbecomingly on the ice, a giggling Alexander on her lap, gazed horrified at the splendid figure in a scarlet tunic, a fur-lined cloak flung carelessly over his shoulder.

'Papa! Papa!' Natasha cried, spinning towards him.

Catherine struggled to her feet, trying to recover her dignity as she led Alexander to the bank.

He was older than the Countess, somewhere in his late thirties. He towered a magnificent six foot, with powerful shoulders and a shock of wavy hair that gleamed gold in the sun and merged into a luxuriant beard. Blue eyes sparkled with zest as he swung Natasha high in the air.

'You seem to be enjoying yourselves, little one.'

'Oh, I am, Papa. I am. Miss Eleanor is a most wonderful skater. She's taught me all kinds of new steps.'

'Then I arrived too late. I saw only the finale!'

Catherine's cheeks burned, but he was holding his hand out to her, beaming as disarmingly as Alexander.

'I see you have made a good beginning with these two rascals. Don't let them bully you. They terrified their French governess out of her life.'

'Mam'selle was no fun,' Natasha protested. 'She wouldn't play.'

'And is Eleanor fun?' the Count asked as she danced around him.

'Oh yes,' Natasha enthused. *'Lots.'*

Catherine took off her skates and tried to regain her composure. The Count swung a squealing Alexander high onto his shoulders and called out lustily, 'Come and say hello to my bear cubs!'

For a bewildered second Catherine wondered who he was talking to and then another figure moved forward from the cover of the snow-laden trees. Like his host he wore knee-high gleaming black boots, his trousers tucked into the tops, the sable coat opening loosely to show a silk-bloused shirt, high at the throat and belted at the waist as Alexander's. Catherine stared at him helplessly.

Her new world was crumbling in ashes before it had begun. He would inform the Vishnetskis that she was a reformed street-walker and she would be dismissed instantly. And she hadn't the fare back to England. Or to her grandmother in France, or anywhere. She squared her shoulders and faced him, waiting to be denounced.

To her amazement, when he stepped forward and took her hand, his eyes registered no recognition whatsoever.

'The childrens' new governess, Miss Eleanor Cartwright,' the Count said, scooping and sweeping Natasha up under one strong arm.

His hand was strong and warm and she felt a tremor run through her body. Why was he not acknowledging that they had previously met? Was he enjoying her discomfiture? Did he intend to prolong it for his own amusement? It would be in keeping with his character for him to do so. Seething with rage and misery she followed in the Count's wake as he led the way back to the house.

His wife's eyes lit up as the Count swung into the salon, depositing Alexander in a yelling heap on the floor.

'My darling, I thought you would never be back,' her plump hand caught his, laying it against her cheek. He bent his head, kissing her gently as Catherine hovered uncertainly at the door, not knowing whether to take the children away or not.

'And Dominic! How lovely to see you again.' She held her arms out towards him and he strode across the room, bending down on one knee at the side of the chaise longue.

'It's been far too long, Maria,' he spoke so gently and tenderly that Catherine was caught off guard. Tenderness was not an emotion she had ever associated with Dominic Harland. His parents had disowned him. London society had shunned him. Catherine had believed she had known why. Now, suddenly, she was not so sure. The man kneeling at Maria's side was not the hardened sensualist of the gossip-mongers. Incredibly she found herself wishing he would speak to her as tenderly. The thought took her breath away. He had humiliated her and used her for his own amusement. The least he could have done aboard the *Gretel* was to acknowledge that not only did he know the Vishnetskis but intended visiting them. His manners were appalling by any standards, and yet . .

She gazed at him, bemused. Why did his presence have this disturbing effect on her? It had never happened so with Robert. With Robert she had felt safe and secure, whilst with his brother . . .

'Will you be staying long?' the Countess was asking as he rose to his feet. '*Do* say you will stay until Dagmar returns. She would never forgive me otherwise.'

He turned, near black eyes meeting Catherine's, holding her fast. 'Verechenko's attractions increase every time I visit it. I shall most certainly make my stay a long one, Maria.'

Catherine felt a tide of colour flood her cheeks. Though ostensibly speaking to the Countess he was really speaking to her. Knowing that in her position as governess she had no way of retaliating no matter how much he baited her. With sudden certainty she knew that he *would* bait her. He would not disclose to the

Vishnetskis that he thought her a woman of loose virtue. He would use the knowledge to afford him amusement. And only seconds ago she had been wishing he would speak tenderly to her! Filled with fury at him and at herself she asked tightly, 'May I take the children now, Barina?'

The Countess nodded and Catherine grasped the children firmly by the hand and swept from the salon, her head high, her heart pounding.

She would have enjoyed the next few days except for the constant presence of Dominic Harland. He hardly looked at her, much less spoke to her, but she was painfully aware of his tall, broad-shouldered figure, strolling in the gardens, talking quietly with Maria, leaving Verechenko in flamboyant evening dress after dinner en route to the opera or theatre. She had spent wakeful hours at night planning crushing replies to his mocking questions as to how she was enjoying her reformed life. He never gave her the chance to give them. Instead of being grateful for his silence, it only served to fan the flames of her fury even further.

Neither did it help to discover that Dominic Harland was an excellent horseman, a superb skater, and a magnificent shot with a gun and, rumour had it, the finest dancer to grace St Petersburg's balls for many a long year. Invitations flooded in from the City's noblest families. Night after night Dominic danced, drank and flirted his way through the palaces of Petersburg. Catherine, spending companionable evenings in the company of the Countess, could only hope the attractions would soon pall and that he would continue his travels she cared not where.

The Count and Countess were kindness itself to her. If it was for his childrens' pleasure nothing was too much trouble for Alexis. The childrens' favourite pastime was toboganning and together with their father and Catherine they would laughingly drag the scarlet toboggans up Verechenko's terrace and zoom down at breakneck speeds towards the frozen lake. The Countess had a chaise longue moved across to the vast windows of the salon so that she could see the exhilaration on the childrens' faces and share in their enjoyment.

Catherine's English clothes, being obviously unsuited to the rigours of the Russian weather, the day after her arrival the Countess had presented her with soft felt boots and a fur coat padded and lined with silk. While the ice held they skated every morning, and soon Alexander was flying about after his sister, giggling merrily every time he fell. Dmitri would take them for drives in their *izvozchik*, a horse-drawn sleigh gaily painted red and blue. In the grounds of Verechenko Alexander liked to ride the horse, a large, placid animal that never went faster than a solid plod no matter how Alexander urged it to 'gallop fast like a troika'. To Catherine's intense relief the Marquis showed not the slightest inclination to join in any of these outdoor pastimes.

Two weeks later, as Catherine was preparing to take the children on their customary canter around the grounds, she was appalled to find him waiting for them in the stables, whip cracking lazily against the glossy sleekness of his boots. Silently she allowed the groom to help her into the saddle, seeing with a sinking heart that the

Marquis had already mounted his coal-black stallion.

'I fear our pace will be a little slow for you,' she said, hoping to deflect him from his intention of joining them.

He shot her a glance and said idly, 'A light canter to see how these two rascals are performing on horseback will be enjoyable enough.'

Catherine's heart began to thud. His hands on the reins were large and strong. Hands that had once held her, holding her against her will with savage strength. She fought to contain her anger. He had made a mockery of a marriage proposal to her. He had insulted her. Abused her. She would *not* fall victim to his charm.

The children were overjoyed at his presence, Natasha showing off as she broke into a brisk trot round the lake.

'I wish we were at Lenskia, then we could *really* ride.'

'Lenskia?' Catherine asked curiously.

'Their summer estate in the Crimea,' a dark rich voice said from behind her.

Catherine closed her lips tightly, determined to give him no opportunity to speak to her again. Unrebuffed he said with infuriating pleasantness, 'You ride remarkably well, Miss Cartwright. Considering.'

'Considering what?' Catherine snapped, stung into reply.

He waved a gloved hand airily, 'Considering your background.'

She reined in her horse, and swung round in the saddle to face him.

'My background,' she hissed, her cheeks flaming, 'is impeccable! Any gentleman would know so instinctively. Only a blackguard could have mistaken me for a woman of . . . of . . .'

'Of easy virtue?' he finished, and there was an unmistakable gleam in his eyes.

Only the presence of the children prevented Catherine from slapping him full across his handsome face. Alexander was slipping perilously sideways in his saddle and Catherine cantered over to him, setting him upright, her back rigidly turned against the Marquis.

'I have the distinct feeling you have been avoiding my presence these last few days.'

'I have my duties to attend to,' Catherine said cuttingly.

'Ah, yes, your duties. So irksome to be at someone else's beck and call.'

He was laughing at her and she hated him. Anguish made her reckless.

'I find nothing irksome at Verechenko save for your own presence!'

He laughed softly. 'Careful, careful, my little governess. Remember your position.'

'I'm not likely to forget it when I have to suffer your insufferable rudeness,' Catherine said bitterly.

'But you must suffer it in silence. As a governess you should be suitably servile. Fortunately for you the Vishnetskis are easy going and not a typical family. Otherwise it would be obvious that the position you fill is not one to which you are accustomed.'

Catherine turned angrily, her voice throbbing. 'For once and for all, I am a gentlewoman and demand to be treated as such! It was disgraceful enough that you should have presumed otherwise, but on learning of your mistake you should at least have had the decency to apologise. So far, sir, you have not!'

'No,' Dominic Harland agreed, not taking his disturbing gaze from her. 'But, as you never offered me a suitable explanation for being alone in the London streets in the early hours of the morning, it was a little difficult.'

'I assure you my purpose was quite legitimate,' Catherine said, aware that her voice was unsteady, that he was so close to her person that she could feel the warmth of his breath on her cheek.

'Then perhaps we could resolve the matter finally and you could explain all.' There was no more amusement in his voice or his eyes.

The horses shifted impatiently. She was filled with an overwhelming desire to confess the truth to him. Perhaps he would be kind to her as he was to Maria. The moment was a pulse beat of time and then she remembered that he had left London rather than honour the proposal of marriage he had made to her. She said icily,

'I was seeking aid from a friend.'

'Aid?' Dark brows rose questioningly.

Their eyes locked and held. The breath hurt in her chest.

'I was being forced into a marriage that was abhorrent to me.'

His honey-gold skin seemed to tighten over his cheekbones.

'My commiserations, ma'am,' he said and swung his horse away from hers, riding hard for the distant pine woods.

Catherine blinked back a sudden onrush of tears. She had achieved her objective and rid herself of his presence, but the day had been spoiled.

That evening, as she descended the stairs to the salon, he was standing in the marble entrance hall, his valet putting final touches to the immaculate folds of his evening cloak. He raised his eyebrows, and this time there was no amusement, no vestige of kindness on his face as he beckoned her with a finger as he might one of the dozen lackeys who waited on the Vishnetskis' every whim. Alexis was entering with Dmitri, slapping him heartily on the back, guffawing at some private joke. In the presence of her employer Catherine had no choice but to obey the beckoning finger. Stiffly she walked across to him, halting some feet away. He was no longer looking at her. His valet was handing him his top hat and cane and as he drew on his gloves he said carelessly, 'I hope you will forgive me saying so, Miss Cartwright, but the substance you use on your hair appears to be fading. It might be circumspect to re-apply it. Good evening.'

Catherine gasped at his audacity, clenching and un-clenching her fists as he strolled out to the waiting carriage, crested with the Vishnetskis' coat of arms.

'Are you happy at Verechenko?' the Count asked kindly as he accompanied her into the salon.

'Yes, sir,' Catherine said between clenched teeth, wishing she could sound more enthusiastic. He treated her as a guest and friend rather than an employee and deserved a more heartfelt reply to his question.

'Good, good.' He settled himself in a high-wing leather chair near to the fire while Catherine took her customary seat near to the Countess's chaise longue.

'You have not seen much of St Petersburg yet, have you? We must rectify that; what do you say, my love?'

The Countess gazed at him fondly, letting her embroidery drop into her lap.

'I was thinking that perhaps when Dagmar returns Eleanor could accompany her to the theatre and the opera.'

'A marvellous idea,' the Count said enthusiastically. 'Dominic was saying only today that he would like to take the children to the Maryinsky. He suggested Eleanor should accompany them as Alexander is so small . . .'

The blood drummed in Catherine's ears so that the rest of the Count's sentence was lost to her. How dare Dominic Harland suggest she spend an evening in his company? Hadn't he insulted and tormented her enough? Did he imagine she would be grateful for such attention? Her mind whirled. One thing was certain. Nothing would induce her to acquiesce to his request. Anger stung her cheeks into flame. She was a governess, an employee. Dominic Harland had no need to request her presence. If he took the children to the theatre then the Count would simply instruct her to accompany them. And she would have to obey.

Dmitri entered the room deferentially. 'Captain Bestuzhev to see you, Count.'

Alexis grunted, rising reluctantly to his feet. As the door closed behind him the Countess picked up her embroidery again and said, 'I do wish Dominic would fall in love and marry. There isn't a girl in St Petersburg who isn't mad for him.'

Catherine would dearly have liked to inform the Countess that there was one young lady in St Petersburg who was not besotted with the Marquis and that only weeks ago the gentleman in question had agreed to marry without the bother of falling in love. Instead she asked tightly. 'Does the Marquis spend much of his time in Russia?'

'A little, but he lives mainly in Paris.'

'What about England?' Catherine asked ingenuously. 'Surely that is his home?'

The Countess flushed slightly. 'There is a rift between the Marquis and his father. Some boyish high spirits many years ago.'

Being fired at by an outraged husband outside the Royal Box at Ascot was hardly to be classified as boyish high spirits. But Catherine was too fond of the Countess to protest, and, after all, she was supposed to know nothing about it.

'I thought things would improve now that his brother Robert is dead,' the Countess mused, laying her embroidery in her lap.

Catherine's needle pricked her finger, drawing blood. She staunched it quickly with her handkerchief as the Countess continued.

'I hadn't seen him for the past five years. Not since my last visit to England, but he was a fine young man. His death was a great tragedy.'

Catherine knew she should be asking what the tragedy had been, but she was unable to speak. Tears hung unshed in her eyes and her throat was tight and constricted.

'They were totally dissimilar, of course. Robert was placid and even-tempered, while beneath Dominic's suave exterior lurks a wildness equal to that of Bestuzhev's Cossacks.' She laughed. 'I suppose that is why he has never married. He would demand too much from a woman.'

'Perhaps the Marquis would not make the best of husbands,' Catherine ventured, unable to say that she thought any girl who married him would have to be clean off her head.

'He would certainly be unmanageable.' the Countess agreed. 'There would be no twisting Dominic around her little finger. But then, is that what a woman wants in a man? Surely it is better to be mastered than to have a fawning lap-dog? I know I would rather have my Alexis, even though he is like a great bear, than any of the effeminate dandies I met in my London season.'

Catherine, remembering Bertie Pollingham, could only agree with her. But only where the Count was concerned. Not the Marquis. The Countess admired him because she did not know the other side of his character. A side that would force a passionate kiss on an unprotected young woman. Who would refer to her openly as a woman of easy virtue and then, discovering his mistake, not even condescend to apologise. The side that would agree to marry, sight unseen, and then jilt the young lady in question, humiliating her before both their parents. There was a lot the Countess did not know about Dominic Harland, Marquis of Clare. Catherine wished heartily that she could enlighten her.

'You will be the focus for much feminine jealousy when you accompany him to the Maryinsky with the children. Not many people will know your true position and there will be much speculation when you appear at his side,' the Countess continued.

'No!' the protest was torn from her.

Maria's gentle eyes were startled.

'I mean, no, I would rather not accompany the Marquis to the theatre.' Catherine said scarlet-faced, realising her rudeness.

Understanding dawned in Maria's eyes. 'So you find our guest as devastating as Amelia Cunningham does?'

'Amelia Cunningham?'

'Lady Cunningham arrived in St Petersburg last week. She is staying with the Nestorevs, but no doubt when Princess Dagmar returns they will stay with us for a short while. Lady Cunningham's daughter is barely seventeen, but Alexis tells me she has eyes for no one but Dominic.'

'Indeed,' Catherine said politely, thinking that Amelia Cunningham showed a sad lack of taste and wondering why she should suddenly have a sick feeling in the pit of her stomach.

'That is where Dominic has gone this evening,' the Countess continued, once more picking up her embroidery. 'He is taking Lady Cunningham and Amelia to see Nijinsky dance.'

Catherine stared bleakly down at her embroidery, noting with mild surprise that she had embroidered both a stem and a leaf in a searing scarlet. Dispiritedly she began to unpick her stitches, wondering how far into the early hours it would be before the Marquis returned from his evening in Amelia Cunningham's company.

CHAPTER
FOUR

THE icy grip that had held St Petersburg frozen ever since her arrival, was beginning to thaw. The next morning as she took the children for their customary walk in the grounds she noticed that the lilac trees were beginning to bud and that the lawns were green under a slight layer of frost. There came the sound of pounding hooves and the Count's troika whirled down the wide drive towards them.

'Papa! Papa!' the children shrieked, running heedlessly towards him. Catherine, terrified they would rush in front of the galloping hooves, gave chase. She need not have worried. The horses were already rearing to a standstill, Alexis leaping down and running to meet his children, crushing them to him as if he had been away for weeks and not hours.

'Where are the well-behaved English children your Mama wants?' he asked, as Alexander clambered all over him and Natasha swung from his neck. 'You are like bear cubs! Russian bear cubs!' And he hoisted Alexander high on his shoulders, sweeping Natasha up in one arm.

'Have you brought me a present, Papa?' Natasha asked.

He cuffed her playfully. 'So . . . you are only pleased

to see your Papa if he has a present for you. What if I have no presents? Are you still pleased to see me?'

'Of *course* Papa! We love you!' and she gave him a big kiss, one arm pressed round his neck, and said, 'But have you a present? Just a very little one?'

He swung her up in the air with a roar that had her screaming with joy and fright.

'No I have not, but I have a surprise for you, a wonderful surprise,' and he set her on her feet, growling as he chased both laughing children across the terrace to the salon.

'Oh what is the surprise, Papa? Please tell us. Please!'

'Captain Bestuzhev is coming tomorrow night with some of his men and is going to give a display of riding and dancing for you.'

'Oh, Papa!' Alexander hugged his father tightly, his face alight with joy. Natasha clapped her hands delightedly. 'Will we have fireworks, Papa, and dancing?'

'If Dmitri can organise the fireworks in time, we will have fireworks,' her father promised.

Alexander crowed with delight. 'Cossacks! Real Cossacks!'

Only his wife did not seem overjoyed at the Count's news.

'What is the matter, Maria?' Alexis asked, noticing a slight frown on her forehead.

She shrugged. 'You know I do not like him, my love. I never have done.'

'He's a Cossack. You can't expect him to behave like an English gentleman.'

'No. But he's so fierce . . .'

Alexis laughed. 'He has to be to keep those men in

check. He's the finest Cossack officer this side of Moscow.' He turned to Catherine. 'Wait until tomorrow, Eleanor. Then you will see a glimpse of the *real* Russia!'

All next day the servants scurried backwards and forwards in a frenzy of activity. To Catherine's relief the Marquis was neither at breakfast nor lunch and was nowhere to be seen either in the house or in the garden. Fairy lights were strung along the terrace and through the trees, barrels of beer were rolled from the cellar and giant tables were laden with food. It was dusk when the earth shook beneath the onslaught of hooves and a score of horsemen galloped down Verechenko's driveway in a cloud of swirling dust. Minutes later the salon doors opened and Captain Bestuzhev was announced.

Catherine's first impression was that he was enormous. He was even taller than Alexis, with bulging thigh muscles and the neck and shoulders of a bull. His great dome of a head was bald and shiny, his mouth unsmiling beneath a drooping, grizzled moustache. He brought into the room a smell of sweat and horses and something else that Catherine could not define. He bent over her hand and she flinched inwardly, understanding Maria's dislike of him. His eyes, half hidden in thick folds of flesh, drifted over her speculatively and then he was accepting a vodka and Alexis was saying to him, 'The children are looking forward to seeing your men ride. It was very generous of you to offer to come.'

Bestuzhev shrugged. 'It gives them a little practice,' he said indifferently, 'We have to perform before the Tsarina soon and the food and drink that you supply for my men is always generous.'

Alexis slapped him on the back. 'Then let's get the party under way. Are you ready, my dear?'

The Countess nodded. Dmitri stepped forward, picking her up into his arms and carrying her out onto the terrace to the waiting sofa. Catherine followed, wrapping a fur carefully around Maria's shoulders and handing her her muff.

Lanterns glowed like fire-flies in the dusk and the small lake gleamed dull gold beneath lamp-lit trees. In the light of flaring torches she could see Bestuzhev mounting his horse and Alexis taking the children to a safe vantage point.

The servants crowded the foot of the terrace steps, chattering in excitement. Alexander swung high on Alexis' shoulders, grasped his father's hair, his face enraptured. Slowly the twenty or so men cantered into formation, the giant-like figure of Bestuzhev at their head. For a few seconds there was complete silence, the murmur of voices dying as they all waited expectantly. Then, upright in his stirrups, Bestuzhev waved his sabre high, uttering a blood-curdling cry to charge. Catherine drew in her breath as with loud whoops men and horses thundered down towards the lake, circling it at full tilt. Like avenging furies they began to gallop back to Verechenko, their long whips cracking menacingly, their faces ferocious in the blood-red glow of the torches. Maria shivered.

'I think I will go in now,' she said to Catherine. 'I can't bear to think of the poor creatures who find themselves on the receiving end of those dreadful whips.'

'They are reining in their horses now. It's nearly over.'

Maria shook her head. 'No, there will be some trick

riding now. I can't even watch that without feeling frightened. Dmitri! Dmitri!'

Dmitri, never far away, stepped forward and lifted her gently in his huge arms, carrying her indoors. Catherine stayed out on the terrace as the Cossacks raced full tilt, swinging, somersaulting, jumping. At last, bathed in sweat and deafened by admiring cheers, they leapt from their horses to be feted with brimming tankards of beer.

As they slaked their thirst the musicians began to play, filling the evening air with pulsating rhythms. Servants and musicians surrounded the Cossacks in a large clapping circle and as the men began to swirl and leap to the strum of balalaikas Catherine ran down the steps to get a closer look.

A laughing Alice made room for her in the circle and she joined in the frenzy of clapping as the music grew faster and faster in time to the mens' flashing boots. Then it was the servants' turn to dance.

Gagarin, the under-butler, grabbed at an unsuspecting Alice, pulling her laughingly after him and whirling her round in wild abandon. The next minute Dmitri had hold of Catherine's waist, and was pulling her protestingly into the centre of the throng, spinning her round and round as the music grew faster and faster, so that the faces around her were nothing but a glazed blur. As the music ended and she gasped for breath, Dmitri forced a way through the crowd, searching for beer.

'My goodness, how do they keep it up?' she asked as the violins began playing and the lawns of Verechenko throbbed to the beat of hands and feet.

'This is nothing. Ask again in six hours' time. Where the devil is the beer table?'

'Below the terrace, next to the musicians.'

Dmitri grinned, his teeth even yellower in the torch-light. 'Wait here while I get myself a glass,' and he shouldered his way through the chanting throng towards the beer barrels.

All around her the embraces of dancing couples were growing more blatant and Kira, Maria's maid, was being kissed passionately by one of the stable boys. Catherine thought it wisest to slip back to the house before Dmitri returned with similar ideas.

She was seconds too late, but it wasn't Dmitri who strode past and gripped her wrist, but Bestuzhev. Polite-ly she demurred, trying to disentangle herself, but Bes-tuzhev wasn't listening. His huge dome of a head was glistening with sweat, his eyes glazed with alcohol. With a bellow he charged into the throng, dragging Catherine after him. To struggle would have been futile and the only escape that Catherine could see was to keep a frantic look out for Dmitri, and to make a dash for it the first time Bestuzhev's hold on her slackened.

Crushed to his massive chest she was pushed and buffeted, the shrieks of the dancers and the racing rhythm of the music deafening her.

At last, just when she felt she could hang on to her self-control no longer, the music ceased and Bestuzhev threw his arms wide, yelling for more. Before he could regain his grasp, Catherine twisted away, pushing be-tween two half-drunk footmen and racing across the lawns as fast as her skirts would allow. By the time she reached the foot of the terrace steps she was breathless. In the distance the torches leaped and flamed, and she could see the unmistakable glint of Bestuzhev's head as he whirled a more willing partner to the throbbing music.

With a gasp of relief Catherine hurried up the darkened steps. As she did so a broad-shouldered figure swung through the open French windows, leaping down the steps two at a time, knocking her off balance so that she fell to her knees.

'What the devil . . .' Dominic said good-humouredly, bending down and helping her to her feet. A firework shot across the night sky and in the golden trail it left behind Dominic saw who it was and the laughter faded slowly from his face.

'Leaving the party so soon?' There was a strange throb in the rich timbre of his voice.

Her heart hammered painfully. 'The party has grown a little too boisterous.' She wondered if he had seen her dancing with Bestuzhev and hoped that he had not.

The singing and dancing was growing wilder by the minute and his eyes glinted.

'So it is. A pity I arrived late otherwise I could have claimed a dance as the Captain did.'

'I had no desire to dance with the Captain,' Catherine said as freezingly as the tremble in her voice would allow. 'He forced his attentions on me.'

'Did he indeed?' Dominic's eyes narrowed. He tilted her chin upwards with his forefinger. 'You will forgive my presumption, Miss Cartwright, but the last time we met in such convenient darkness I had the distinct impression that my attentions were not altogether unwelcome, despite your later protestations. I wonder if I was right?' And before she could resist, he had pulled her firmly towards him, kissing her full on the mouth.

She beat her hands frenziedly against his chest, fighting against every instinct that urged her to succumb, to wind her arms around his neck and knot her fingers in the tight, black curls.

His lips seared hers, burning and bruising. Without the strong support of his arms she would have fallen. She could no longer breathe, her heart was beating so painfully, the blood pounding through her veins. There was a strange light in his dark eyes as he finally released her.

'You are . . . insolent!' she gasped, blinking back a surge of hot, humiliating tears.

'You are bewitching,' he said, and his eyes were bold and black and blatantly appraising.

She gave a strangled sob and slapped him across the face with all the strength that remained to her, running blindly inside as he stood, one hand to his face, watching with a curious expression in his eyes as she disappeared into the chandelier-lit rooms.

Catherine ran along the crimson-carpeted corridors to her room faced with a bitter truth. She did not hate Dominic Harland. Her feelings for him were far more turbulent. Far more disturbing. Was it possible she was in love with him? A man she had left England rather than marry? A man who had left England rather than marry *her*? She lay on her bed and stared into the darkness with anguished eyes.

All through the night she tossed and turned restlessly. She was under no delusion that Dominic's kiss had meant anything to him more than another chance to humiliate her. If only she had taken Caroline's advice and stayed to meet him . . .

But then, she thought savagely, pummelling the pillows, he wouldn't have been there *to* meet. What if she had gone immediately to Geddings and confronted him before he had left? Would that have made any difference? Would he have reconsidered then?

A fresh wave of misery swept over her. He wasn't in love with her now, so why should he have fallen in love with her then? Only now it was worse. Now he thought her a woman of light virtue. She wasn't at all sure that he believed her explanation for being alone in the London streets in the early hours of the morning. And seeing her dance with that great oaf Bestuzhev would have only reinforced his opinion.

She stared sleeplessly at the cherub-encrusted ceiling. As a governess he would never entertain any serious ideas about her no matter what she did. She wondered if Amelia Cunningham was pretty. Springing from the bed she lit the lamp and surveyed her hair in the mirror. Dominic had been right. The dye was fading, the copper-coloured glints showing clearly. With her hair its natural colour she would stand far more chance of attracting his admiration, but how to explain to the Countess that she had had it dyed?

Despondently she climbed back into bed and tried to sleep, but even in her dreams he followed her: sensually aware, mockingly confident. Worst of all, indifferent. When she woke she felt as if she had not slept at all. Heavy-eyed and weary she took the children downstairs to the salon.

Outside the salon doors Olga waited, fat arms folded across her bosom, black silk straining at the seams.

'It is *my* turn to take the children this morning,' she

said triumphantly as Catherine approached.

Puzzled, Catherine halted, a child held by each hand.

'Every month *I* take the children to Cheka, *my* village.'

'Then I must see the Countess,' Catherine said reasonably.

Olga laughed, showing small, crooked teeth. 'Come to Olga,' she said, bending down towards the children.

Alexander pouted. 'Don't want. Want to stay with Eleanor.'

'Now come along, Barinushka,' Olga coaxed, 'You come with old Olga.' Olga pulled him towards her.

He tried to wriggle free. 'Want Eleanor,' he persisted. 'Love Eleanor.'

Olga's eyes hardened, her grip tightening.

'Do as you are asked,' Catherine said gently to him, sensing another scene. 'And I will go into Mama and make quite sure that today is the day you are going to Cheka.'

Reluctantly the children stayed with Olga while Catherine entered the salon.

'I'm sorry I didn't warn you before, Eleanor,' Maria said, laying down her book. 'I quite forgot with the hurly-burly of yesterday. But each month Olga and Dmitri take the children to Cheka. It is on our estates but a good twenty versts from Petersburg. They won't be setting off till eleven, but it will give you enough time on your own to see something of the city without having the children at your heels.' She picked up her book again, saying as an afterthought, 'Oh, by the way, the Cunning-hams are coming to stay. I had a telegram from Princess

Dagmar saying the Crimea is boring and that she can't wait to get back to civilisation. The next few weeks should be quite hectic!'

With mixed feelings Catherine went back to a gloating Olga.

'The children will be ready for you at eleven.'

Olga's eyes narrowed, her smile disappearing, but Alexander's face lit up with joy.

'Does that mean we can go fishing first? There's no ice left on the lake now.'

'If you go straight away,' Catherine said indulgently.

Alexander clapped his hands. 'I *love* fishing. I caught ever such a big fish last year. If I catch a big fish today can we have it for dinner?'

'Of course we can. But it will have to be a very *big* fish if we are all to have some.'

'Then I'll catch two. Two *giants*!'

The morning sun held a hint of warmth as they ran down across the lawns to the lake, Alexander pretending to be a Cossack and charging on ahead of them like a wild thing. Natasha chattering happily.

'There is a big fish over there,' Natasha said, as they settled themselves on the bank of the lake. 'It must be a carp. There it goes! Look!'

Alexander gazed goggle-eyed and would have fallen in the water if Catherine hadn't caught hold of him.

'Sssh. We'll never catch fish if you make all that noise,' she remonstrated.

'Caught one!' Alexander yelled. 'I've caught one! Quick! Quick! Don't let it get away!'

He was so beside himself with excitement that Catherine hadn't the heart to suggest he throw it back and steeled herself to take the poor wriggling creature off the hook.

'Two,' she said severely. 'Only two. Any more must go back in the lake.' By the time they set off back to the house with Alexander's proud catch, Catherine had almost forgotten the unpleasant news of Amelia Cunningham's arrival. Laughing and singing they made their way back up the gentle slope, the children running eagerly on ahead to show their prize to the cook and to make quite sure it would grace the dinner table. None of them saw the watching figure on the balcony.

Dominic's face was inscrutable. Then, as Catherine raised her eyes and saw him he turned curtly on his heel and disappeared into the room behind him.

If she had any last lingering doubts as to the motive behind his kiss, they vanished abruptly.

The children disappeared with Olga and Dmitri, Alexander's chubby little arms clinging around Catherine's neck as if he would never see her again. For weeks she had longed for the opportunity to explore St Petersburg. Now she no longer had the heart for it. A footman hurried across to her.

'The Barina requires your company, Barishna.'

From behind the closed salon doors came the sound of strange voices and laughter and then the unmistakable sound of Dominic's deep voice. Her stomach muscles tightened into an uncomfortable knot as the footman bowed slightly and flung open the carved doors.

A massive lady dressed in hideous purple sat on Catherine's customary chair beside the Countess. Steel grey hair showed beneath a broad-brimmed hat crowned with a mass of ostrich feathers. Pince-nez hung on a golden chain around her neck and she picked them up, peering at Catherine with a disapproving expression as she entered.

'My governess, Eleanor Cartwright. Eleanor, Lady Cunningham.'

Lady Cunningham received Eleanor coldly. She had no very high opinion of governesses. She returned her attention to the Countess and enquired for news of the Tsarina's health.

Catherine sat down, avoiding Dominic's eyes, her pulse beating alarmingly. At the window a girl her own age stood admiring the gardens and the lake. She was smaller than Catherine, a mere five feet with a face like a kitten's. Cornflower blue eyes smiled seductively beneath delicate brows, her nose was short and straight, her chin finely moulded. Cherry-red lips pouted prettily, but Catherine thought she detected signs of sulkiness in the spoilt, pampered face. The Marquis seemed to have no such qualms. There was no mistaking the admiration in his eyes as he leaned nonchalantly against the mantelpiece, a small smile playing on his lips as their eyes met over Lady Cunningham's oblivious head.

'Amelia is so looking forward to seeing Karsavina dance,' Lady Cunningham said, turning to face Dominic.

'I shall be more than delighted to escort her, ma'am,' Dominic said, his eyes still holding Amelia's.

Amelia lowered her eyes modestly, but the satisfied smile on her lips did not escape Catherine's notice. She was growing more and more sure that Amelia Cunningham was not the shrinking violet she was trying to appear. She was out to ensnare Dominic and why he hadn't the sense to see that . . .

The footman swung open the doors hastily as Alexis strode into the room. 'My dear Lady Cunningham; my dear Amelia! Well, well, this is an honour. Sherry? Or is it too early? Perhaps some tea. Igor! Lemon tea at once!' He rubbed his large hands, as his valet relieved him of his cloak. 'So, what news from England, eh? What rumour of war there?'

Lady Cunningham did not trouble with rumours of war, only fashion. 'The King was in excellent spirits when last I saw him.' She didn't deem it necessary to explain that this had been at a considerable distance. Count Vishnetski was a close intimate of the Tsar and it pleased her to give the impression that she too enjoyed her sovereign's friendship.

War. It was the first Catherine had heard of it. She said, without thinking, 'What war do you mean, sir?'

Lady Cunningham gave her a frozen stare. The Marquis scrutinised his gleaming toecaps and Alexis, seeing nothing untoward in Catherine taking part in the conversation said, 'Trouble in the Balkans. The old Kaiser is getting mighty fidgety. Bestuzhev thinks that there will be war before the year is out.'

'Bestuzhev?' Lady Cunningham didn't recognise the name, but then prime ministers were not her forte.

'Captain of a crack Cossack regiment,' Alexis said, disillusioning her. 'He has bet me a thousand roubles the Russian and French armies will be meeting in Berlin this summer.'

Amelia, bored, tapped her foot impatiently and tried to win Dominic's attention again. She failed. It was centred entirely on Alexis.

'I hope you win your bet, Alexis. I doubt that Russia is equipped for war.'

'Oh, stop talking about boring old war,' Amelia said pettishly. 'Is it true that the Tsarina no longer attends public balls? I do *so* want to see her. I believe the balls in St Petersburg are much grander than those in London. I do *so* enjoy dancing, don't you, Dominic?'

She spoke his name intimately, as if it was well-known to her. As well it might be, Catherine thought jealously, seeing the secret looks that passed between the two of them.

'There is nothing I like better,' the Marquis agreed smoothly. 'I am sure you will take St Petersburg by storm.'

She laughed prettily and Catherine had an overwhelming desire to kick him savagely on the leg. What on earth was he doing making a fool of himself over a simpering, scheming little minx like Amelia Cunningham? Dominic's reputation was that he was immune to female charms. He certainly wasn't acting as if he was immune to Amelia's. The conversation continued interminably, only Alexis throwing her a friendly smile now and then as she sat with hands folded demurely on her lap, eyes downcast, the picture of a perfect governess.

When at last the Cunninghams took their leave and Alexis and Dominic had left for the Count's club, Maria said to her, 'Isn't Amelia a pretty child? Perhaps there's hope for Dominic yet.'

Catherine remained silent with difficulty.

'I do hope you will forgive me if I sound rude, Eleanor, but there is something I should like to mention to you.'

Catherine stiffened, wondering what *faux pas* she had committed.

Maria laughed. 'Don't look so worried my dear. You've done nothing wrong. I'm more than pleased with you. It's just that . . .' She hesitated awkwardly, then said with a rush, 'It's just your hair. It appears to be changing colour.'

'It is,' Catherine said despairingly. 'You see, I dyed it and now I don't know where to go for any more hair dye . . .'

Maria threw her head back in a peal of laughter. 'Good heavens, child, why on earth did you dye it? It's a glorious red. I can see quite clearly on the crown and every day the whole length of it takes on a more coppery colour. Why on earth cover it with a drab dark brown?'

'I . . . I . . .' Catherine struggled vainly.

Comprehension dawned in Maria's eyes. She patted Catherine's hand. 'I understand. Governesses are to be mouse-like and discreet. Not raging beauties who might catch the eye of the master of the house. Put your mind at rest. I would much rather have a raging beauty in Verechenko than a brown mouse. Not,' she added, 'that you could pass as a mouse, no matter *what* colour your hair was. I am conceited enough to believe that Aphrodite herself could not steal my Alexis from me. So no more hair dye.'

'Thank you, Barina.' Catherine's thanks were heartfelt. She was not a vain girl but to have deliberately concealed her main claim to beauty had been hard. Especially under the circumstances. Perhaps if she washed her hair repeatedly the dye would fade quickly.

When the Countess dismissed her she made straight for her room and surprised her little maid by demanding jugfuls of hot, soapy water.

CHAPTER
FIVE

THE next morning Catherine surveyed the results critically. Rich red hair gleamed with its old health. She
brushed it into a chignon, and left a few stray tendrils
about her forehead and cheeks. It was fashionable to
wear it short now, but nothing would have persuaded
Catherine to cut her waist-length locks. They were her
crowning glory and she knew it. Her eyes, too she
thought, studying them impassively, were certainly not
commonplace. Like her grandmother's, they were a
brilliant green, tilting slightly at the corners, alight with
laughter and a love of life. At least they usually were.
This morning they gazed back at her from the mirror,
troubled and confused.

What was she doing? Struggling to make the best of
herself to gain the admiration of a man who thought her
little more than a slut, a man who had behaved insulting-
ly by any standards. Yet perhaps she was doing him a
great disservice? What if he had left London after
learning that she, Catherine, had fled? Wouldn't that
put a different complexion on things? If so, he had acted
honourably.

A close and loyal brother to Robert, he had offered to
marry and take care of his bereaved fiancée. She forgot
entirely her remarks to her step-mother when *she* had

84

attributed such motives to him. Yes. Dominic had acted
quite nobly and she had exposed him to public humiliation. Although no engagement had been officially
announced Catherine knew her step-mother well
enough to be sure that her coterie of friends would have
been well aware of the drama being enacted between the
Davencourt and Harland households and of Lady
Davencourt's expectations of becoming mother-in-law
to a future Duke. One, as she had so openly put it, who
owned half of Southern England. If that was the case it
put a whole new light on the matter.

Throughout the day Catherine saw Dominic intermit-
tently, either deep in conversation with Alexis or striding athletically across the lawns to the lake. Once he
entered the salon while she was sitting with the Countess
and the children. She had felt as though her heart would
burst within her as he passed so close that her skirt
brushed against his leg. But he had given her only the
slightest of nods, his eyes scarcely registering her presence.

All the while he was in the room she watched at close
quarters the honey-coloured skin, the fascinating lines
that deepened around his mouth as he laughed with the
Countess, the ease and assurance of his stance, the
broad shoulders beneath the scarlet silk Russian tunic.
The clothes of the country suited him. The trousers
tucked into glossy knee-high boots. The short fur-edged
cape that swung jauntily from one shoulder. It was hard
at times to remember that he was an Englishman so well
did he fit into his present environment. She wondered if,
in Paris, he would be indistinguishable from a Parisian
and doubted it. There was something subtly Russian

about Dominic Harland. A brooding restlessness mixed with sudden laughter and flashing, devastating smiles.

She tore her eyes from his uncaring figure. No wonder he had never fitted into London society. He must have been like a cuckoo in the Harland nest: Robert so quiet and responsible. Dominic so volatile and unpredictable.

Her throat felt tight and dry. What if she told him who she was? That she had fled to Verechenko rather than marry a man she did not know. Surely in this day and age her action had been reasonable enough? But then he would argue that at least she could have been courteous enough to meet him. He certainly wouldn't believe she was being *forced* to accept his marriage proposal. Her step-mother could be charm itself when necessary. Her behaviour in leaving in such melodramatic circum- stances had been childish and had humiliated him. If he knew who she was any hope she entertained of gaining his affections would be at a complete end.

He continued to behave as if she were no longer in the room and Catherine's emotions were in a turmoil. It was like being on a giant see-saw. Why should she *want* his admiration? Had she suddenly become weak in the head? She remembered the burning pressure of his mouth against hers. Or a wanton? She should be avoid- ing his presence, not seeking it out. Her head ached with confusion.

'And so Princess Dagmar will be in St Petersburg by noon,' Maria was saying happily.

'Is she still the same?' Dominic asked.

Maria laughed. 'Princess Dagmar *never* changes, Alex- is says she's impossible, but then blood relations never have much tolerance with each other, do they? I must admit that she can make life difficult if she chooses. The trouble is, she has no suitable companion to accompany her to the theatre and concerts. She has no patience with her contemporaries and most of the young women who would be eligible to act as companion to a princess of her rank she regards as foolish idiots. *And* tells them so!'

Dominic laughed. 'I know another lady of similar temperament in Paris. She solved the problem by dispensing with a female companion and enjoying the company of eligible young men who welcome her wit.'

Catherine's eyes were still downcast and she did not see that he was looking at her as he spoke.

'Princess Dagmar would eat half the young men in St Petersburg for breakfast,' Maria said with amusement. 'They don't have enough backbone for her.'

'Then perhaps I should stay in the background,' Dominic said drily. 'I should hate to be eaten, even by Dagmar.'

Maria laughed. 'Don't be silly, Dominic. You have the backbone of ten men. I just wish you would settle down and marry. Alexis tells me you have been squiring the pretty new dancer from the Maryinsky about town. Is it true?'

'I'm not a monk, Maria,' he said fondly.

Unknowingly Catherine's hands tightened in her lap.

'*Please* try and behave for my sake,' Maria was saying scoldingly. 'Amelia Cunningham obviously adores you and she would make an ideal wife for you.'

'You think so?' The Marquis appeared to be giving it deep thought. 'Then perhaps I should send her red roses. That should make my conquest complete.'

The light mockery was back in his voice and Maria

said, 'You're funning me, Dominic Harland, and I won't put up with it. Alexis told me himself that you were contemplating marriage.'

'*Had* been,' the Marquis agreed equably.

Catherine felt the colour rise in her cheeks like a tide. Of all the conversations to have to be a silent party to! She wished the ground would swallow her up. She was saved further embarrassment by the footman opening the door and announcing, 'Countess Nestoreva's carriage has arrived for you, sir.'

Dominic kissed Maria's hand in goodbye and without the merest glance in Catherine's direction he left the room.

The Nestorevs. Where the Cunninghams were staying. No doubt Amelia Cunningham was there now, waiting to simper and flirt once more with him.

The doors opened once again and the footman, this time with his usual calm slightly flustered, announced, 'Princess Dagmar, Barina.'

A wizened figure, weighed down by ropes of waist-length pearls, entered the room. Her dress was of powder-grey lace, her face wax-white with make-up, the only colour the blood-red of the rubies adorning her fingers. In one hand she carried a silver cane. Catherine wondered why. It obviously wasn't necessary to assist her to walk. She was soon to find out.

She kissed Maria briefly on both cheeks. 'I hear we have that rascal Harland with us. Should liven things up a bit. The Crimea was like a cemetery. It was a fool idea going at this time of the year. Marquis of Clare now is he? Would never have expected it. The older brother was only in his late twenties, wasn't he? On the quiet side

if I remember rightly. Would have made a most respectable member of Britain's upper classes. This one won't,'
she cackled. 'Probably marry an opera singer and upset
the lot of them. Serve 'em all right. Too fuddy-duddy,
the English. No blood in their veins. Who asked that
damned awful Cunningham creature to stay? Can't
stand the sight of her. Looks like a camel but hasn't that
animal's brains.'

'She came because of you, darling,' Maria managed to
interrupt at last.

'Then she needn't have bothered. Shan't have anything to do with her. Who's that?' Piercing black eyes
stared at Catherine, looking her up and down as though
she were a chattel.

'Eleanor Cartwright, the governess Mrs Oversley re-
commended.'

'Doesn't look like a governess to me,' the Princess
said frankly, staring at Catherine's thick titian hair and
up-tilted eyes.

'No, she doesn't,' Maria replied agreeably. 'She's very
pretty. The children adore her and so do I.'

'Umph.'

The Princess tapped her cane imperiously on the
floor. 'Come here, girl. Let's have a closer look at you.'

Torn between amusement and apprehension Catherine approached the diminutive figure.

'Well, you're a beauty all right,' she said at last,
grudgingly. 'So you're Eleanor Cartwright?' she asked,
and there was a gleam in the black eyes that Catherine
found distinctly unnerving.

'Yes, Your Highness,' she wondered if she should
curtsey and decided that she had better.

'Then if you're going to be part of the fixtures and fittings I'd better get to know you. Come on.'

With a swish of lace on the floor and a careless tap of her cane on the footman's shoulder as she passed, she left the room.

Catherine gazed confusedly at Maria who smiled encouragingly. 'Do as she says. And stand up to her. She doesn't like to be fawned over.'

A stout, flustered figure in a too-tight pale blue satin dress, was hastily bade to one side as the Princess made her royal progression up the sweeping flight of stairs, preceded by the liveried footman and with a small negro boy in scarlet tunic following some yards behind. Up the magnificent staircase, turning right down the deeply carpeted corridor through room after room that Catherine had never entered before, until at last they came to a high-ceilinged salon of eighteenth-century elegance. The female companion, for such Catherine assumed her to be, hung nervously about at the door to be dismissed with a wave of the cane. The footman bowed deferentially. The doors closed. The Princess seated herself in a rose-pink velvet covered chair, tapped her ruby-encrusted fingers on a glass-topped table and said without preamble, 'The strangest people visit the Crimea.'

'Yes, Your Highness.' Catherine wondered if perhaps the Princess was slightly mad.

'The Grand Duchess was there of course. And there was a smattering of English and French. Met an English Dowager Countess of French extraction with hair remarkably like yours. Eyes too, now I come to think of it. She was recuperating from a fall. *I* knew her when I was a girl. Wasn't a member of the British aristocracy then,

but they could do with more like her. Called herself
Gianetta Dubois in those days. You wouldn't know who
I'm talking about by any chance?'

Catherine stared at her like a rabbit at a fox. The only
person who knew where she was, was Gianetta. She had
written to her immediately, asking her not to disclose
her whereabouts to her parents and explaining the
reason for her flight. She had not wanted to cause
anxiety to her dearly-loved grandmother and her trust in
Gianetta had been rewarded. There had been no com-
munication from England to Verechenko. But now her
grandmother had forsaken the Riviera for the Crimea.
And had fallen into friendship with the Princess. Not
surprising considering the similarities in character of the
two old ladies. As the enormity of what had happened
sank in, the room reeled and Catherine sank, unasked
into a chair. The Princess did not comment on this
amazing lack of etiquette, merely continued to stare at
her with eyes like black shiny pebbles.

She would have to leave Verechenko. The daughter of
Lord and Lady Davencourt could hardly be retained as a
governess. And Dominic would discover her true
identity. His indifference would deepen into contempt.

'I hate liars and hypocrites,' the Princess said crisply.
'So perhaps we could have a little truth.'

'Yes,' Catherine's voice was a mere whisper as she
tried to collect her thoughts.

'Are you Gianetta Dubois' granddaughter?'

If she admitted it, she would never see Dominic again.
And seeing him, even in the company of Amelia Cunningham, was suddenly preferable to not seeing him at
all. Her eyes met the Princess Dagmar's.

'Yes,' she said, two large tears sliding down her cheeks. 'Yes, I am.'

The Princess threw back her head in a gale of laughter. When she recovered sufficiently, she said, wiping streaming eyes, 'And do you mean to tell me that my thick-headed nephew never suspected?'

'No, Your Highness, I made a very *good* governess.'

'I'm sure you did.' She cackled appreciatively. 'And what did you do when that young cub Harland arrived?'

'Nothing. I . . . It was very awkward,' she finished lamely.

'I'll bet it was!' The Princess rubbed her hands together in sheer enjoyment. 'So . . . You flee to Verechenko to avoid meeting him and he turns up on your doorstep. What do you think of him, now you've seen him? A handsome devil, isn't he?'

'He's . . . I mean . . .' Catherine floundered.

'Come on, girl, I won't give you away if you don't want me to, but have the grace to allow me to enjoy this situation to the full. Life's dull enough when you're eighty. So what did you think when you met him? That you'd been a hot-headed fool and should have stayed?'

'*He* didn't stay.'

The Princess's brows, plucked to such a thin line that they were almost non-existent, flew up.

'*He* left England the same way I did,' Catherine continued indignantly. 'He hadn't the slightest intention of marrying me. He was amusing himself, that's all. Making a fool of his parents and of me.'

'Is that so?' The Princess leaned forward, hands clasped around the top of her cane. 'And how would you know a thing like that?'

'Because we travelled on the same boat,' Catherine said bitterly.

The Princess's eyes narrowed speculatively. 'Oh yes, and what happened between the two of you on the boat? Come on, child, I'm not in my dotage. I haven't enjoyed myself so much for years, and I don't want cheating of any of it. What happened?' the Princess waited expectantly.

At last Catherine said despairingly, 'He thought I was a woman of easy virtue.'

This time the brows disappeared completely and an expression of unalloyed delight spread over the heavily-powdered face. 'A *cocotte*!' It was all the Princess could do to stop herself clapping her hands in joy. 'Now what on earth gave him that idea?' Her expression changed suddenly. 'You haven't . . .'

'Of course not,' Catherine said indignantly. 'It was nothing to do with my behaviour on the boat. It was before.'

The Princess hung on every word. 'Before?' she asked impatiently as Catherine seemed reluctant to continue. 'What happened before?'

Catherine sighed. It was obvious that she was going to be able to keep nothing back from the sharp-witted Princess.

'My step-mother told me I had no choice as to whether I married Dominic. She said she would make my life unbearable if I refused and I knew her well enough to believe her. So, before she could carry out her threats I decided to run away to my grandmother who was in Paris at the time. I had no money of my own and so I slipped from the house late at night when no one would see me, and went to the Oversleys'. I knew Caroline Oversley had plenty of money and would lend me what I needed. A man followed me and stole my purse and then . . .' She shuddered descriptively. 'Dominic heard me scream. He punched the man to the ground and then sent him reeling with a kick of his boot down the alley.'

The old lady chuckled.

'I thanked him and he then had the arrogance—the gross impertinence—to suggest that I change my profession before I got hurt or murdered!'

The cane was rammed appreciatively into the floor as the Princess hunched her shoulders, leaning forward even further, anxious not to miss a word.

'Then, on the boat, when I told him I was a governess, he congratulated me on taking his advice!'

This was too much for the Princess. She rocked backwards and forwards with laughter, tears streaming down her face, while the footmen outside the doors looked at each other in wonderment.

'And then?' the Princess managed at last. 'And then? When he met you here?'

'He *knew* I was coming here!' Catherine said angrily. 'I told him so on the boat and he said only that he was "acquainted with the Vishnetski family", not that he would be staying with them. That man,' she added heatedly, 'has a very *warped* sense of humour!'

'So he thinks you're a reformed street-walker?'

'I've told him that he's wrong!'

'And did he try to take advantage of the fact? A full-blooded man like that. Come on, child. What happened?'

Catherine pursed her lips, and the Princess tapped her

cane impatiently. 'Come on, don't be so old-fashioned. I thought you were Gianetta Dubois' granddaughter. What did the rogue do?'

'The night in the alleyway, when I thanked him, he kissed me.'

'He did, eh? And since?'

'When the Cossacks came to ride for the children it was dark and I fell on the terrace steps. He helped me to my feet and . . .'

'Kissed you again,' the old lady finished with satisfaction. 'So . . . What's the difficulty? You're *not* a governess or a cocotte, so why don't you want him to know who you are?'

'He didn't kiss me out of affection,' Catherine protested. 'He simply took advantage of me. He's totally ignored me otherwise. He spends all his time making eyes at Amelia Cunningham or taking some dancer out from the Maryinsky.'

Catherine's green eyes blazed. The Princess chuckled. 'And you don't like it, eh? Well, why not tell him the truth?'

'Because I'm not *sure* why he left England. I said it was because he had no intention of marrying me, but what if I'm wrong? What if his intentions were perfectly honourable and he knew I had run away rather than marry him? My step-mother is an awful gossip. The whole of London will know he had been publicly jilted. It's hardly likely to endear me to him, is it?'

The Princess was thoughtful. 'So that's the position, is it? You're not sure? Well then,' she settled herself back in her chair. 'We'll not tell Alexis who you are. *He* wouldn't keep it a secret. And I'll have a private word with that young devil and find out the truth of the situation. Though why on earth you couldn't marry the man your father chose for you I cannot imagine.'

'I didn't love him then, Your Highness,' Catherine said ingenuously, giving herself away.

'I didn't love my husband but I married him,' the Princess replied spiritedly. 'Were you never tempted to tell Alexis your true identity? It can't have been easy acting the part of governess.'

'I was afraid that if I did so he would feel morally obliged to tell my father who I was.'

'Well you needn't worry about that with me. I never felt morally obliged to do anything in my life. But I'm going to enjoy sorting out this tangle. I'll have a word with Dominic at the first opportunity.'

Impulsively Catherine rose to her feet and kissed the Princess on the forehead. The old lady smiled, saying gruffly, 'Run along child. I'll have a word with Maria too. It won't harm those two scamps to do without a governess for a week or two. Olga has a face like sour cream and I suppose that is your doing. I need a companion and from now on that's what you'll be. You shall have to have new clothes and some jewellery. Can't have you wandering round St Petersburg looking like an impoverished milkmaid. I'll get Kiril to advise me on stones. Emeralds, I think, with that hair. I shan't tell Kiril either. This could be interesting. *Very* interesting. Run along child. I'm tired. I'm not used to such excitement all in one day.'

The bizarre behaviour of the Princess in purloining the children's governess and turning her into friend and companion did not take the Vishnetski family or servants by surprise. They were used to Princess Dagmar's eccentricities. Only Alexis was annoyed, complaining that when they had finally got a competent governess who could both control and teach the children, and one they loved into the bargain, Dagmar should so high-handedly steal her from under their noses.

'It's only for a few weeks,' Maria had said soothingly. 'And it would be marvellous for Eleanor to see the other side of St Petersburg. The glamour and the beauty. It will be like a fairy-tale come true from her.'

Though English-bred she shared none of her country-women's stiff regard for protocol. It appealed to her romantic nature to envisage a simple girl, used to nothing more than governessing, entering the dazzling world of St Petersburg society.

For Catherine, born into one of England's noblest families, the transition was an easy one. But even she found some of the luxury that was enjoyed by the Princess startling. She was surrounded continually by a vast army of maids and menials who pampered to her every whim. She affected elbow-length white kid gloves for afternoon visiting. Every day a new pair, French made, soft as velvet, was brought tissue wrapped by her personal maid. Catherine wondered where the discarded pairs, worn so briefly, disappeared to.

There was a servant whose sole duty was to unroll a strip of deep-piled crimson carpet from the entrance of Verechenko to the Princess's carriage every time the Princess left for a drive, and to perform the same service at her destination. The little negro boy, turbanned like an Indian, was always in discreet attendance, a bowl of fresh fruit continually at the ready for when the Princess should desire a peach or one of the out-of-season oranges that came direct from warmer climates. There were maids whose only duty was to fill the Princess's marbled bath tub with steaming, rose-scented water. Maids whose only duty was to care for her vast collection of jewels. Maids who dressed her entirely from top to toe. Never once had the Princess Dagmar ever deigned to pull on her own stockings.

As her companion, Catherine found her own little maid dismissed, to be replaced by two rosy-cheeked girls, expert at the elaborate coiffures that were needed to enhance her new collection of dresses. After weeks of wearing the sensible dresses she had brought with her to Russia, the dresses that the Princess showered her with were a delight.

There were suits for daytime made by Worth of Paris, the long, tight skirts emphasising her slender hips. A tunic was worn over the top, reaching to just below the knee, swinging voluptuously as she walked, and there were little hats that perched on top of her fiery hair, beautiful feathers projecting at a jaunty angle. There were evening dresses by Paquin, delights of silk and chiffon and lace. There were even harem trousers of fine satin to wear visible beneath the hem of evening skirts as worn by members of the Russian Ballet. There were afternoon dresses in pale pinks and lilacs, draping softly over her bosom and hips, the sleeves fastened with row upon row of tiny pearl buttons. There was a lace confection in the softest green that had a small Medici collar at the back, plunging in the front to a V-neck. It was so revealing it would have shocked her step-mother into a stupor, but Princess Dagmar, surveying the high, rounded breasts, nodded approvingly. There were fox furs and sables, ropes of pearls to twine in her hair and box after box of exquisite kid gloves. Within hours Catherine's boudoir was a treasure house as the Princess's orders were hastily carried out.

Catherine hardly recognised herself as she looked in the mirror to see a vision in deepest lilac, a single camellia still sparkling with the dew of the Crimea from where it had arrived, tucked demurely at her bosom. Vilya, her new maid, had been enraptured at the red-gold waist length hair it was now her privilege to dress. She had arranged it in a crowning profusion of gentle curls. Soft tendrils escaped as if by accident to enhance Catherine's youth and vulnerability.

With her heart pounding nervously Catherine stepped out into the chandelier-lit corridor and down to the salon. Tonight she was to accompany the Princess to the Nestorevs and she knew that Dominic was entertaining the Countess in the main salon. Tonight he would see her in her new role for the first time. She anticipated the expression in his eyes as he saw her, her vibrant beauty no longer obscured under the guise of serviceable dresses and restrained hair-styles. Apprehensively she allowed the footman to throw open the doors and entered the main salon where Maria, imprisoned on a chaise longue held court.

A silence fell on the cluster of resplendently-dressed people gathered in the salon. All eyes were on Catherine as she stood framed by the two liveried footmen. Alexis drew in a deep breath of undisguised admiration and the Princess's eyes gloated with satisfaction. The dumpy, frizzy-haired woman who had hovered around the Princess on her arrival was also there, as was a gentleman Catherine had never seen before. He stood, tall and erect, behind the Princess's chair. If Catherine had looked at him she would have seen that he had a face handsome enough to turn any girl's head. Blue eyes fringed by thick, gold-tipped lashes, fair hair brushed sleekly, a clipped moustache above well-shaped lips. But she was not looking at him and did not see that he was gazing at her with a spell-bound expression on his face. She was conscious only of Dominic.

He stood a little apart from the others wearing the scarlet tunic and gold braid of Alexis's regiment of which he was an honorary member. Catherine thought she had never seen any man look so magnificent. She could forgive him anything if only he would love her a little. She waited for the shock; the realisation that must surely dawn in the dark secret depths of his eyes. There was none. His eyes rested on her fleetingly and then returned to the Countess as he continued his conversation. Her disappointment was nearly too much to be borne. Digging her nails deep into the palms of her hands she sat on a gilt and velvet chair and strove for outward composure.

'Eleanor is accompanying Dagmar to the Nestorevs this evening,' Maria was saying to Alexis and Dominic.

'If her entrance there has anything like the effect it had here it should be an evening to look forward to,' the Princess said with relish. 'What are you dithering for, Lena?'

'I don't think Lena and Eleanor have been introduced yet,' Alexis boomed, striding forward and taking Catherine by the hand.

'Eleanor, my dear. Baroness Kerenskaya, another member of our household.'

'For our sins,' the Princess said audibly behind him.

'And Lixy Korrosky.' A slim boy of seventeen or eighteen stepped forward and took her hand, kissing it lightly.

'Take no notice of Lixy,' the Princess said rudely. 'No one else does.'

There was a gleam of laughter in Lixy's eyes. 'Delighted to meet you, Mam'selle.' His smile was sincere and Catherine decided then and there that no matter who he was, she liked him and felt instinctively that she had found a friend. She wondered what relation he was to the Princess, but the Princess did not trouble to enlighten her.

'And my grandson,' the Princess said carelessly. 'Prince Kiril.'

The suave and exquisitely dressed Prince took Catherine's hand, pressing it to his lips. There was no gleam of laughter in *his* eyes. Only an expression that sent a tingle down Catherine's spine. If only Dominic would look at her like that. If only she could inspire some emotion other than amusement or bland indifference.

'My pleasure, Mam'selle.' He held her hand for longer than was necessary and Catherine was uncomfortably aware of Maria's interested gaze. Dominic was no witness to the Prince's obvious admiration. He was staring out of the tall narrow windows to where the trees in the vast grounds rose darkly in the moonlight.

'Fedya delivered your bauble to me by mistake,' the Princess said to her grandson, waving her cane at a ring box on the nearby table.

'Fedya's a fool,' he said, reaching a hand out for it. 'In future I shall patronise only Fabergé.'

The Princess chortled. 'Then start tomorrow. Eleanor needs some jewels.'

The Prince gazed across at the creamy complexion and luxuriant coppery hair. At the sea-green eyes seductively uptilted at the corners.

'Eleanor needs no jewels at all,' he said, hardly able to take his eyes away from the tantalising breasts and slender hips. 'She's a jewel in herself.'

Maria laughed. 'Very prettily said, Kiril.'

The Princess showed not the least displeasure at her grandson's obvious admiration for her protegée. 'Pretty words are all very well. But you must take her to the jewellers in the morning, Kiril. Emeralds, I think. But see what Fabergé says.' Then, changing the subject entirely, she said abruptly, 'When is the coming-out ball for the Grand Duchess?'

'There isn't going to be one,' Kiril said, finally tearing his eyes from Catherine's face.

'Not going to be one!' The silver cane was rammed violently into the carpet. 'Olga is eighteen! There *must* be one!'

Kiril shrugged. 'Apparently not. The tercentenary celebrations have exhausted the Tsarina and she feels unequal to the effort.'

'I'm beginning to think those girls are nothing but a figment of my imagination! It's months since I saw one of them!'

'The Tsarina looked distinctly ill the last time I saw her,' Dominic interrupted mildly.

'Then she's no right to be ill,' the Princess said unreasonably. 'What is the use of a Tsar if he hides himself away all the time? He barely uses the Winter Palace now. It's an eternity since the last ball. Even the Dowager Empress told me that she has encouraged the Tsarina to take more part in public life, but it makes not the slightest difference. She stays cooped up at Tsarkoe Selo sticking reams of photographs into reams of albums. The only person she *does* listen to is that wretched monk. Have you seen *him* these last few weeks?'

Dominic shook his head. 'No, nor want to if all I've heard is true.'

The Princess shuddered. 'This conversation is depressing me. Let's see your ring, Kiril.'

Carelessly Kiril flicked open the lid. Catherine gasped. A magnificent sapphire glittered on a bed of black velvet. Even Maria gasped with pleasure.

'Not bad,' his grandmother said grudgingly. 'Can't stand sapphires myself. What does it look like on?'

To Catherine's dumbfounded amazement Kiril walked slowly across the room, lifted her hand and slipped the ring on to her index finger.

'Very nice,' his grandmother said without flickering an eyelid, 'and better there than on the hand of some opera singer. Come along, Eleanor, the Nestorevs will be waiting.'

Deferential footmen helped the Princess and Catherine into a polished and gleaming Mercedes with the Vishnetski coat of arms emblazoned on the doors. Silently they sped through the crowded St Petersburg streets and squares. Carriages were taking people to theatres, restaurants, receptions. The men wore flowing evening cloaks lined with scarlet silk; the women beautiful osprey feathers and diamonds in their hair as they walked from their carriages towards the glittering entrance halls. On arrival at the Nestorevs the Princess waited impatiently while the red carpet was unrolled and she regally descended.

'The Cunninghams will be here,' the Princess said to Catherine as they were led past a huge jardinière of hot-house roses and ferns and up a marbled sweep of staircase.

'This is their last evening before they come to Verechenko. Alexis must be weak in the head inviting them.'

Catherine felt her pulse quicken. What would the Cunninghams make of her transformation from governess to companion? The Princess had an air of anticipation about her as they were formally announced and Catherine knew with sudden certainty that it was because she knew Catherine's presence would shock.

The dining room was candle-lit, the table enormous. On each chair of dark red leather the Nestorev's coat of arms was embossed in gold, and behind each chair stood a white-gloved footman.

Even Catherine felt a little sorry for Lady Cunningham's obvious confusion as she was reintroduced to Eleanor as Princess Dagmar's friend and companion. That Russians were barbarous Lady Cunningham had long suspected. That they were mad she now knew beyond a certainty. Countess Nestoreva, anxious to please the notoriously difficult Princess, and knowing nothing of Eleanor's history, greeted her charmingly, sitting her next to a gentleman old enough to be her grandfather, glad that her son was absent this evening, at least until she had ascertained just who the incredible beauty was that Princess Dagmar had so suddenly found.

Also sitting at the magnificent table was Count Nestorev, an elderly gentleman who dozed off at regular intervals, and a young man who was obviously Amelia Cunningham's escort for the evening.

Amelia stiffened on seeing Catherine arrive as a social equal, and in a dress that could only have come from Paris. Every eye was turned in Catherine's direction. Her hair was glorious, piled high in a confection of red-gold curls, interlaced with pearls: a single, perfect camellia at the bodice of her gown drew all eyes to her beautiful breasts, and Amelia nearly choked with fury and envy. Icily she ignored Catherine, determined at the first opportunity to enlighten Countess Nestoreva as to the true class and position of the girl flaunting herself so boldly among her betters. That her escort seemed mesmerised by Catherine and found it difficult to pay attention to Amelia's own ceaseless flow of inane conversation, only incensed her further. If that brazen hussy was parading around Verechenko in front of the Marquis of Clare in such finery . . . Amelia's lips tightened. She had set her heart on becoming the Marchioness of Clare and Dominic's attentions to her had convinced her that they would be affianced before she left St Petersburg.

Countess Nestoreva, happily oblivious of the tension among her guests, cooed indulgently to Catherine, 'And that *delightful* young Marquis! I had hoped he would be able to join us this evening. So handsome, so charming, yet so . . .' Plump shoulders rose expressively, '. . . so *dangerous!*'

'The Marquis is a particularly close friend,' Lady Cunningham said between spoonfuls of kissel. 'In fact, I have every expectation that our relationship will become even closer.'

The Countess's eyes widened, as she looked at Amelia.

Lady Cunningham's eyes met Countess Nestoreva's and the Countess, aware of the presence of Amelia's present escort, said no more. It was unnecessary. Lady Cunningham had been perfectly clear. So that was who her little guest had set her heart on. Countess Nestoreva, who had played hostess to the Cunninghams for eight weeks, wished the Marquis well. In company Amelia Cunningham was all that could be asked of a young lady. Sweet and pretty, her soft voice tinkled with laughter as she hung on to her escort's every word. In private Countess Nestoreva had discovered she was a bad-tempered, spoilt and selfish girl. She would not be sorry to have her guests leave. She doubted if Amelia would be able to give vent to her tantrums in the Vishnetski household, not with that old dragon Dagmar in residence.

Catherine had no further appetite. Lady Cunningham would never have made such a blatant insinuation unless there was some truth behind it and she had seen herself the way Dominic had looked at Amelia when she had visited Verechenko. Whatever Princess Dagmar's intentions, they were going to be too late. She felt slightly faint. If anyone had told her a few months ago that love could be this senseless, desperate longing she would have laughed at them and accused them of reading too many romantic novels. But now there wasn't a waking moment when she didn't crave for Dominic's presence. And Amelia Cunningham, sitting opposite her, avoiding her like a leper, would be able to claim his presence morning, noon and night. The feeling of faintness increased and she was barely conscious of the Princess saying,

'So you'll be arriving at Verechenko tomorrow, then?'

'Yes,' Lady Cunningham agreed, thankful that the temperamental Princess was at least being civil.

'The Marquis is calling for us himself at ten o'clock. Such a *well-mannered* young man.'

Catherine, remembering the side of Dominic that only she knew, grimaced, her finger unconsciously touching her lips, feeling again the pressure of his mouth against hers. The sapphire flashed in the candle light and Amelia gave a little hiss as she saw the magnificent stone for the first time. Catherine was unaware of it. All she could think of was how she was to endure the next few weeks, seeing Dominic continually in Amelia's company. It was too much to ask anyone to bear. For the first time she considered leaving Verechenko voluntarily. Going as she had planned to her grandmother: trying to forget. But even as the thought came to her she knew it was impossible. She must be near him, no matter what the cost to her pride. The kissel tasted of sawdust. She lowered her spoon, her hand motionless on the table, willing the evening to be over so that she could seek the sanctuary of her room, and escape Amelia Cunningham's vicious blue eyes.

CHAPTER
SIX

THE next morning felt strange to Catherine. There were no laughing, tumbling children to wake her. Maria had been adamant that for the next few weeks at least she was to be in no way responsible for them. She had, in Maria's own words, to give herself up to enjoyment. If that meant more evenings like the previous one Catherine doubted she had the stamina to endure them.

Vilya helped her into a dark-green day dress, the long tight skirt moulding itself around Catherine's narrow waist and slender hips. The sapphire flashed on its bed of black velvet. The Princess had insisted that she wear it. Today Kiril was to take her to Fabergé and more jewels would follow. Reluctantly she slipped it on her finger. It was still early. The Princess, Vilya informed her, would not rise before noon. The children had gone to Cheka. The Cunninghams were due later in the morning.

Pensively Catherine wandered down the magnificent staircase and out onto the terrace. Verechenko's vast army of servants hurried silently about their business. Spring had come to St Petersburg and there was the sweet smell of lilac in the air and the new leaves on the trees surrounding the ornamental lake were a glossy, lush green. Slowly she walked down the steps, one hand running down the stone balustrade. She paused on the step where she had fallen and where Dominic had carelessly helped her to her feet, reliving again the moment when his eyes had registered her identity and flooded with an expression that had left her weak.

Desolation swept over her. He would never have treated Amelia Cunningham in such a cavalier manner. To him she was at most a governess. At worst . . . She bit her bottom lip. No wonder he felt free to kiss her whenever he pleased and ignore her the rest of the time. Wasn't that how a lady of loose virtue would expect to be treated? Never having met one Catherine did not know, but suspected that it was. She walked on, the dew wet grass dampening the hem of her skirt as she continued across the lawns to the lake.

'Good morning,' a bantering voice said and Catherine turned with a start, seeing with a mixture of relief and disappointment that it was Lixy leaning against the trunk of a tree, blowing cigar smoke skywards in a purple haze. 'How did you enjoy your visit to the Nestorevs last night? I hope the Princess was not completely impossible.'

'Not completely,' Catherine said with a smile.

He grinned. 'She can't stand fools which makes her circle of friends a small one and limits visiting relations alarmingly.'

'Are you a visiting relation?' Catherine asked, no one having bothered to enlighten her as to the reason for Lixy's presence at Verechenko.

'No. I'm simply a friend of Kiril's.' He paused, 'And you?'

'I know the Oversleys who are friends of the Vishnetskis',' Catherine said truthfully.

Lixy blew another fragrant cloud skywards and did not pursue the subject. It was common knowledge that before their arrival Eleanor had been acting as governess to Alexander and Natasha. Yet she was obviously at home in the milieu the Princess had so suddenly set her down in. And he had seen the way his friend, usually so immune to female charms, had been affected by her beauty. It was all most intriguing.

Swans glided past, leaving a shining ripple of water in their wake. They watched them companionably, at ease in each other's company.

'Had you met the Marquis before?' Catherine asked, unable to stop herself.

Lixy's eyes widened fractionally. So that was the way the land lay. He could tell by the slight tremor in her voice and her effort to appear careless of the answer.

'No, but he is an old friend of the family's.'

'Do you know anything about him?' Catherine ventured.

'A little. His brother died tragically at the beginning of the year. Until then he lived mainly in Paris. Something of a black sheep I believe. But now he has inherited the title and is the only heir.'

'Strange that he did not go back to England under the circumstances,' Catherine kept her eyes fixed firmly on the swans.

'He did. I believe he intended to marry, but there was a scandal and he left as hurriedly as he arrived.'

The blood thundered in Catherine's ears. 'A scandal? What kind of a scandal?'

'Nothing to distress you, Mam'selle. Clare's behaviour was beyond reproach. For reasons known only to himself he decided to marry his brother's bereaved fiancée.'

'And?' Catherine could hardly bring herself to ask the question.

Lixy shrugged. 'The young lady in question agreed and according to her mother, Lady Davencourt, a date was fixed. Do you know the Davencourts? I've heard the first Lady Davencourt was a beauty, but her successor is a Tartar! Anyhow, Lady Davencourt broadcast the news far and wide and the young lady in question fled. Not only that, but her maid said she had called the new Marquis a dissolute, odious womaniser whom no decent girl would marry. And *that* unfortunately found its way into the papers. All the old scandal that had surrounded him in his youth was resurrected. The papers had a field day as you can imagine.'

Catherine felt violently ill. 'And so he left?'

'Oh, he left before it became public news. The minute he knew his offer of marriage was unwelcome he apologised to the Davencourts and took a ship to St Petersburg. I can't say I blame him. The Davencourt would have made a terrible mother-in-law, and the daughter sounds a prig of the worst kind. The least she could have done was thank him for his offer and not make him look every kind of a fool.'

'Yes.' It seemed to Catherine that her voice came from a vast distance. The questions she had been tormenting herself with had been answered. Under no circumstances could she now reveal to him who she was.

'He must have loved his brother very much,' she managed at last, 'to offer to marry his fiancée.'

'Very much,' Lixy agreed soberly, and then in an

effort to cheer her, said, 'But no doubt he was relieved at not being obliged to go through with his offer. Now he can marry for love.'

'The Countess thinks that might happen very soon,' Catherine said, wondering if Lixy also knew anything about the relationship between Dominic and Amelia Cunningham.

'I believe it could,' Lixy said, thinking he was offering her encouragement, and wondering how Kiril would take having the only female who had kindled any response in him whisked away from beneath his nose and under his own roof.

Despondently Catherine took his proffered arm and accompanied him back to Verechenko. At last she knew the full situation, the public scandal her thoughtless behaviour had caused. The sun shone, the birds sang, and Catherine wished heartily that she was dead. She thought of the heartbreak it must have caused Dominic's mother, who had always been so sweet to her. The shame she had brought upon herself. And bitter as gall was the knowledge that a marriage born out of Dominic's sense of honour and responsibility would have brought her a joy deeper than any she had imagined in her wildest dreams. For that she could have made Dominic love her she had not the slightest doubt. The desire was there. She had seen it in his eyes. If he knew her to be socially equal, even if he knew her to be a governess but respectable, she was sure she could have won his love. But he thought her a woman of light virtue and treated her accordingly. And if she had ever had any temptation to reveal her identity so that his assumptions would be proved groundless, Lixy's words made sure she never gave way to it.

Unnoticed by either of them Kiril was watching from the balcony. He stood, legs astride, his hands resting on the stone balustrade, his deep blue eyes admiring. The English girl was a delight. That supple body with the high, firm breasts and soft swaying hips. He wondered if she was aware of the tantalising seductiveness of her walk and doubted it.

She was an enigma to him. The flashing green eyes and red-gold hair indicated a passionate nature, as did the full, generous mouth, yet there was an air of vulnerability about her, an uncertainty that intrigued him. The Prince, a connoisseur of beautiful women and used to their adoration, was aware he had evoked no response in his mother's companion. She had seemed scarcely aware of him. His eyes lingered on her mouth. He longed to kiss those tempting lips, longed to find out for himself the depths of abandoned response they were capable of. He studied the perfect oval of her face, the high cheekbones and creamy smoothness of her skin. There wasn't a girl in St Petersburg to compare with her, certainly not the irritating Amelia Cunningham with her ceaseless flow of chatter and fluttering lashes.

Yet no one knew who she was. Although she had been acting as governess to Alexander and Natasha, the Prince had never for a moment believed that to have been her real function. She was too obviously well born, and there had been no chastisement from his grandmother when he had impulsively presented Eleanor with the sapphire. His infatuation was obvious and his grandmother had done nothing to dissuade him. If the girl had been nothing but a governess there would have been

harsh words and a painful scene over his behaviour. So
. . . who was she? And why was she here? The mystery
only enhanced her attraction.

He had never desired a woman before with such
intensity, yet Dominic, well-known for his string of
female conquests and the broken hearts that lay in his
wake, showed not the slightest interest in her. Prince
Kiril felt something like relief. Lixy he could handle.
The Englishman would have been competition of quite
another kind.

'You enjoyed your walk?' the Prince asked cour-
teously.

Lixy grinned, aware that his friend was severely put
out at his escorting Eleanor alone around the lake.

'Beautiful,' he enthused wickedly. 'The swans, the
birds singing: all very romantic, Kiril.'

'Yes. I'm sure it was,' Kiril said, resisting the temptation to cuff Lixy's ear. He turned to Catherine and
smiled. 'The carriage is waiting when you are ready,
Eleanor.'

'The carriage?' Catherine had completely forgotten
about the arranged trip to Fabergé.

Behind Kiril the French windows were closed against
the chill of early morning and in the room beyond
Catherine could see a familiar head, face thoughtful as
he listened to Alexis who was drumming his huge knuck-
les on his desk, and showing Dominic a mass of papers.
Her heart missed a beat. If he raised his head he would
see her. Surely he could hear their voices?

'This way,' the Prince was saying, escorting her gently
but firmly back down the terrace steps and round to the
front of the palace where the coach, emblazoned with

the Dolgorovsky coat of arms, waited.

'But my coat?' Catherine protested vainly.

Even as she spoke a little maid dropped a pale sable jacket around her shoulders and handed her long kid gloves that matched the colour of her dress exactly.

Not daring to give a backward glance she slipped her long fingers into the soft gloves and only Lixy was aware of how reluctant Princess Dagmar's companion was to be given free rein in the treasure house of Fabergé. He had seen the way her eyes had been drawn to the windows and knew as well as she who stood beyond. A pity, Lixy thought to himself, as he watched the coachman help them into the carriage. The Marquis of Clare's reputation had preceded him and he had never embarked on any affair with seriousness. Eleanor could get herself hurt there, and he liked her too much to want that to happen to her. Whereas Kiril's interest in her distinctly exceeded that he usually showed in a pretty face.

In Lixy's estimation, Kiril was on the verge of falling in love, if he hadn't done so already. And if Lixy was any judge of character, and he flattered himself that he was, then it would be with the full approval of his grandmother. As not even the visiting German Princess last year had found favour in Princess Dagmar's eyes, Lixy found the whole situation tantalising. And in another few hours there would be the added complication of the arrival of Lady Cunningham and her daughter. Two beautiful women under the same roof: one a fiery redhead, the other a feather-brained blonde. Life was beginning to prove very interesting. He wondered if

Amelia Cunningham had any aspiration to be a Princess or if she would be satisfied with becoming a Marchioness. Either way, the sparks would fly. Lixy lit himself another cigar and pondered the situation, feeling wise beyond his years.

Kiril had been aware of the faint flush in Catherine's cheeks as she took his arm, leading her down the flight of stairs towards the carriage. So he *did* have an effect on her after all. He smiled to himself, aware that tall though she was her head still scarcely skimmed his shoulder and that she carried with her the elusive scent of gardenias. So she was not going to betray her emotions openly. With long-standing experience Kiril knew that once she had been decked in necklaces and tiaras of diamonds and sapphires, and had braclets of emeralds encircling her fragile wrists, and sapphire ear-rings to match the stone on her finger, then she would be unable to conceal her feelings for him and those delectable lips would be his for the taking. And not only her lips: Kiril felt a flood of heat in his loins. Young, unmarried English girls were notoriously difficult to seduce, mainly because they were permanently accompanied by over-protective Mamas and companions. But Eleanor had no such protectress and he knew with an instinct as old as time itself that she was a creature of passion.

With difficulty he controlled his imagination and said, 'My grandmother insists on keeping you a mystery, Eleanor. Am not I permitted to know any more about you than the others? Believe me, I would guard your secret with my life if you so wished.' His voice was gentle and caressing.

'There is no mystery, Your Highness. I came as

governess to the children and now act as companion to Princess Dagmar.'

Kiril laughed. 'I'm not such a fool to be taken in by the governess story, and don't refer to me as "Highness". The name is Kiril: and yours is Eleanor?' There was a question in his voice.

For a moment Catherine wondered if the Princess Dagmar had told him the truth and he was teasing her, then he added, 'Strange. You do not look like an Eleanor. An Eleanor should be a shy, brown-haired, quiet creature: not a girl of such ravishing beauty that she takes men's breath away.'

There was no banter in his words. As he looked across the intimacy of the carriage to her, Catherine knew the compliment had been intended. The expression in the vivid blue eyes deepened.

'You *are* beautiful, Eleanor.'

'Thank you,' Catherine wondered how far it was to Fabergé, aware that with each lurch of the carriage as it avoided a speeding troika or crowd of pedestrians, Kiril's knees briefly touched her own. Despite the spring sunshine the carriage was closed, increasing the feeling of closeness. The hands on his lap were well-shaped, a magnificent diamond on his little finger. Her first impression of him had not been wrong. Even at such close quarters Prince Kiril Dolgorovsky was an exceedingly handsome man, despite the girlish prettiness of his fair hair and gold-tipped eyelashes, there was no denying his blatant masculinity. Yet even in such close proximity he did not make her heart beat the faster, nor her senses reel.

Kiril's fair handsomeness was lost on her. She craved

thick black hair, clinging in tantalising curls in the nape of an olive-toned neck. Broad shoulders that wore a cloak with arrogant panache. Mocking dark eyes beneath sweeping black brows.

The four white stallions were reined to a halt. The customary red carpet was unfurled. The Prince gave Catherine his arm and proceeded to buy her more jewels in one hour than her family had ever possessed in its whole history.

Deferentially they were escorted to a private room, a procession of impassive-faced assistants coming at a clap of hands, with satin cushions bearing an Aladdin's Cave of jewels. Catherine gasped, touching a gold and diamond bar brooch reverently, her eyes widening at the necklaces and pendants. Every so often as the glittering display was paraded in front of her, Kiril would nod his head very slightly. A sapphire and diamond *trois fleur* pendant with sapphire drop ear-rings to match her ring was discreetly packaged in a velvet-lined case. A diamond pussycat pendant with emeralds for eyes followed. An emerald and diamond *petite fleur* pendant joined it. Then an emerald surrounded by diamonds hanging on a fine gold chain. A ruby and diamond heart on a gold chain. The gold and diamond bar brooch. Gold butterfly ear studs and last, but by no means least, a dazzling diamond and coral necklace.

A dazed Catherine tried to make up her mind which was the prettiest, which to choose, and stared unbelievably as package after package was carried by uniformed assistants out to the carriage and the waiting Dmitri.

'*All* of them?' she asked increduously. 'You can't possibly buy me *all* of them!'

'A mere handful,' Kiril said with something like regret. 'They will design a collection of jewels for you personally, but that takes time. These little trinkets will have to do in the meantime.'

'But I can't accept presents as costly as this!' Catherine protested. 'A pendant or a brooch yes, the Princess can't have meant you to buy all *these*.'

Kiril shrugged. To say that he had charged the sapphire and diamond pendant and the gold and diamond brooch to his own account would only cause a fresh outburst of protest and he believed Catherine was quite strong-willed enough to refuse to accept them if she knew from whom they came. He said, 'I'm a far better judge of my grandmother's intentions than yourself, Eleanor.' He smiled down at her, enjoying her pleasure, pleased to have her on his arm. It gave him a heady sense of intoxication that he hadn't experienced since his youth.

As the carriage made its way back through the crowded St Petersburg streets to Verechenko, Kiril grew thoughtful. What he had said, about being an accurate judge of his grandmother's intentions, was true, and he was beginning to suspect very strongly that Eleanor figured very high in his grandmother's intentions for his future. It was a prospect that failed to alarm him. He gazed across at her, her lovely face still bemused by the wealth that had been showered upon her.

'You are very beautiful,' he said at last, as the carriage rocked gently over the broad bridge spanning the Neva.

She flushed slightly, not accustomed to the flirtatious banter that she felt the Prince was indulging in, then she saw the expression on the finely-chiselled face and her confusion deepened.

'Thank you,' she said simply, looking out to where the steel-grey waters swirled below them.

Very slowly he leant across, taking her hand in his. 'I made a mistake in taking the carriage for our excursion,' he said huskily. 'The Panhard would allow me to sit next to you with much greater comfort, perhaps even to . . .' He leaned across to kiss her and she shrank back, withdrawing her hand hastily.

'Please, Your Highness . . . Kiril . . .'

He hesitated. With any other woman he would have ignored her protests with gentle firmness. Especially a woman he had just spent thousands of roubles on. But this one was different. This one was an unknown quantity and for the first time in his twenty-five years, Prince Kiril Dolgorovsky was unsure of himself. He leaned back, surveying her thoughtfully so that she did not know where to look, and then said: 'If I were to tell you that I have fallen in love with you, would you believe me?'

'We've only just met,' Catherine said, wishing that Dmitri would drive faster and reach Verechenko, so putting an end to her embarrassment.

'Sometimes one meeting is all it takes.'

She remembered her meeting with Dominic in the darkened London street. Hadn't she fallen in love then? She'd never been the same since, haunted by his face and voice, longing for his touch.

'I can see by the expression on your face that you agree with me.' Kiril's voice was thick with desire. With every fibre of his being he longed to take her in his arms, yet if she should resist . . .

'I think Lady Cunningham has arrived,' Catherine said with relief as their horses galloped down Verechenko's gravel drive.

Kiril silently cursed Dmitri for not having the sense to extend their ride, then helped her down from the carriage to be greeted by the chime-like laugh of Amelia Cunningham.

'Dear Prince, *there* you are. We thought you were quite lost.' She ignored Catherine as if she did not exist.

'Our trunks have just been taken upstairs. Would you believe we only have thirty-six between us? It makes me feel quite a pauper. But I've decided to travel very light and stock up my wardrobe in Paris on my return.'

'Which is when?' Kiril asked, good manners keeping the hope from his voice.

'Not for a *very* long time,' Amelia said coyly. 'In fact I love St Petersburg so much I could quite happily live here for the rest of my life.'

Faithless too, Catherine thought furiously as she excused herself and made her way to the Princess's boudoir. She had flirted with Dominic till he had been taken in by her and now, the minute his back was turned, she was doing her best to charm Kiril in the same manner. She wondered what Amelia Cunningham's reaction would be if she knew the eligible Prince Kiril had just made a declaration of love to the Vishnetski children's ex-governess. The thought was enough to dispel her fury and make her giggle. It would serve the Cunninghams right if she pretended to reciprocate Kiril's feelings. Then they would *have* to be civil to her.

'That Cunningham creature has arrived,' the Princess

said curtly. 'Why she should count me as one of her friends I can't imagine.' She turned from her dressing-table mirror. 'Let me see what Kiril has bought for you.'

Footmen entered the room, the exquisitely wrapped packages carried on silken cushions.

The Princess surveyed the jewels approvingly and said slyly, 'I suppose you want to know what I've found out about our handsome guest.'

Catherine's smiled faded. 'I've already been told all I need to know. I spoke to Lixy this morning.'

'I see.' She pursed her lips, ruby-encrusted fingers curling round the knob of her cane. 'So what do we do? Announce you at lunch as Lady Catherine Davencourt and put the Cunninghams in their place, or keep up this masquerade?'

'It got into the London papers,' Catherine said, her face scarlet with shame. 'The maid overheard me and talked. She said I had called him dissolute and a woman-iser and that I had said no decent girl would ever condescend to marry him.'

'And did you?' the Princess asked interestedly.

Miserably Catherine nodded. 'And so, of course, they dug up all the old scandal. It must have been dreadful for the family.'

'They'll survive,' Princess Dagmar said philosophical-ly. 'They've survived worse scandals than that in the past. I was there when that hothead attempted to shoot Dominic within yards of the Royal Box.'

Catherine's eyes darkened in misery. Who was the woman Dominic had risked scandal and the wrath of an outraged husband for? Had he loved her very deeply?

The Princess was already rising and as maids fluttered

round and liveried footmen hastened to open the doors, Catherine accompanied her down to the terrace where aperitifs were being served.

The Cunninghams and Dominic turned as the Princess made her entrance, and Lady Cunningham rushed over to her, arms outstretched, skin sagging as she clasped Dagmar's hands in an ecstasy of welcome.

Amelia, torn between a Russian Prince and a wealthy Marquis was doing her best to flirt equally with each.

Trying to be unnoticed Catherine walked quietly towards the balustrade, staring down towards the lake, painfully aware of Dominic only yards away from her.

'What happens when the clock strikes twelve?' his deep-timbred voice asked mockingly.

She drew in a deep, quivering breath and turned to him with outward calm.

'I'm afraid I don't understand.'

He leaned negligently against the balustrade, his eyes roving over the exquisite French-made dress, the choker of pearls that the Princess had insisted she wear, the carefully coiffeured hair.

'I think you understand very well.' A corner of his mouth curved in a crooked smile. 'Last week a brown-haired, demure governess; this week a titian-haired beauty taking St Petersburg and a prince by storm.'

'Why have you to be always so rude?' Catherine asked hotly.

The dark eyes sparked with a light she hadn't seen before.

'Why do you have to be such fun?' he said.

Lady Cunningham called his name. He ignored the summons. When his hand reached out for her she was powerless to resist. His lips brushed her ear, her cheek. She was trembling, his without any reservation. Lady Cunningham's voice pierced the dizzying vortex she was falling into. He released her. Turned. Re-entered the room.

She leaned against the balustrade, her breath ragged, her limbs weak. It was the Baroness who came to her aid. 'It is very selfish of Dagmar to keep you all to herself. Now come and sit next to me at table and tell me all about yourself,' Lena said, oblivious of Catherine's distress.

'The seating arrangements are already made,' Kiril said smoothly as they were ushered in by a white-gloved footman and Catherine was seated next to him.

Dominic's attention was completely taken by Amelia Cunningham on his right and Lady Cunningham on his left. Catherine watched in agony as blonde curls brushed provocatively against his shoulder. He had been toying with her. Already she was forgotten. She blinked back hot, humiliating tears and tried to concentrate on what Kiril was saying to her.

Any hopes she had that he would seek her out again after the meal were in vain. He disappeared in the Vishnetski carriage with Alexis, Lady Cunningham and Amelia. It was an arrangement that was repeated several times in the following weeks as Alexis squired his guests around St Petersburg, and Catherine continued to nurse her bruised heart and spend her time with the Princess.

The afternoons were mainly spent accompanying her in the open landau when she paid visits to elderly friends in Petersburg, or in the polished and gleaming Panhard when she went farther afield, both chauffeurs and cars lavishly embellished with the Dolgorovsky coat of arms. The evenings were a round of parties, theatre visits and concerts. There was Chaliapin at the Aleksandrisky Theatre; there was Pavlova and Nijinsky at the Ballet; there were Wednesday night symphony concerts at the open-air concert hall at Pavlovsk. Catherine's eyes searched for Dominic's distinctive figure wherever they went, her life a misery as she was crushed with disappointment if she did not see him, and suffered torments when she did. His bare-shouldered escort was always the coquettish, kitten-faced Amelia, her arm proprietarily through his as she giggled girlishly up at him through thick-fringed lashes and pouted prettily at his every comment.

CHAPTER
SEVEN

ALTHOUGH it was impossible to catch more than a fleeting glimpse of Dominic, Kiril was constantly present. Never before had Princess Dagmar's grandson spent so much time with her. Surely he would not want to spend another summer afternoon at the elderly Countess Bezobrazov's? his grandmother would ask slyly.

'Not at all,' Kiril replied, well aware of the amusement he was causing her. 'I find her conversation riveting.'

'Now that,' the Princess said, allowing her maid to clasp a choker of diamonds around her throat, 'I find strange. Before you said she was the greatest bore imaginable, and that nothing would induce you to spend even an hour in her company.'

'I was a fool,' Kiril replied, refusing to rise to the bait. 'She has great wit and charm.'

'Fiddlesticks. The only thing that rivets you is Eleanor. Have you told her you love her yet?'

Sometimes even Kiril found his grandmother's outspokenness an embarrassment.

'My private affairs are my own,' he said tightly.

The Princess gave her inimitable cackle. 'Maybe, maybe not, but take my advice. If you love her make sure of her soon. Otherwise it may be too late.'

His eyes narrowed, watching her closely as her maid

put the final touches to the heavy white make-up.

'Too late? But she's not being escorted by anyone else, though God knows half of Petersburg is dying for the chance. It can only be that she prefers my company. You would, I presume, *allow* her to be escorted by someone else if she so desired?'

'That depends on who the gentleman is,' the Princess agreed, surveying the results of her maid's handiwork critically in the mirror.

'But you won't tell me who she is?'

'She's good enough for you to marry,' his grand-mother said bluntly. 'That's all you need to know . . . for the moment.' She rose, putting an end to the conversation and leaving Kiril staring thoughtfully out of the window to the lawns and woods and the distant spires of St Petersburg.

Kiril knew his grandmother too well not to take notice of what she had said. She had insinuated he might lose Eleanor unless he acted quickly. Which meant there was another man. For the life of him he couldn't think who. Vladimir Yurovsky had been sending flowers to her daily, but as far as he knew had not received any response. And that fool Leon appeared at every func-tion Eleanor and his mother attended, ogling her as if she were a creature from another world. For a fleeting moment he wondered if Lixy was his rival and dismissed the idea. Lixy wouldn't dare! Dominic? Kiril frowned. It couldn't possibly be him. He had shown not the slightest interest in Eleanor, but then that in itself was suspect. No man could be in the same room as her and retain the same pulse rate, yet the Englishman gave all his atten-tion to Amelia Cunningham. It was no use going to

Alexis for advice. Alexis knew nothing at all about women except that he had the best wife in the world. Though how that great bear of a man had ever won the gentle Maria was a mystery to Kiril.

He frowned. Was he prepared to ask a woman about whose background he knew nothing to marry him? It was still customary for princes of his rank to ascertain that prospective wives had the *seize-quartiers*, that parents and grandparents and great-grandparents all had noble blood. Perhaps that was why his grandmother was keeping her identity a mystery from him. If his love was deep enough, Eleanor's antecedents would not matter.

He wondered yet again if he loved her. Certainly he desired her. The frank openness of her eyes, completely without guile. That curving mouth that promised so many delights, and the flowing curves of her body that drew his eyes like a magnet. She had made it quite clear that she was going to allow him no liberties. If he wanted her he would have to marry her. And he wanted her.

Purposefully the Prince strode out on to the terrace. In the distance, half shaded by the trees, he caught a glimpse of pale lilac muslin and a gleam of copper curls. His mind made up, Kiril strode quickly down the gravel paths between the formal rose gardens, then broke into a run as he reached the lawns that sloped down to where Catherine stood, watching the swans.

Catherine's thoughts were far from Kiril. The more she saw of Dominic, no matter how fleeting the sight, the more certain she was of her own heart. But he made not the slightest effort to seek her out, and mixed with the love she knew she felt for him was an overwhelming anger. Seeing him pay attention to the bird-brained

Amelia gave Catherine an overwhelming desire to box his ears. Sometimes she didn't know which desire was the strongest. To kiss him or to hit him. It was all very confusing and shadows were beginning to appear around her lovely eyes as she spent sleepless night after sleepless night trying to rid her mind of the vision of Amelia Cunningham in a white lace dress, with a train six yards long, and Dominic, Marquis of Clare, at her side.

'I thought I'd find you here,' Kiril said, trying to catch his breath after his run and to appear his normal, suave self.

'I like it here. You could be miles deep in the country, not in the middle of a city.'

'You like St Petersburg?'

'Yes.' If Dominic was in it then of course she liked it. If he had been in Siberia then no doubt she would have thought Siberia the pleasantest place on earth.

'You would enjoy living here?'

'I enjoy living here at the present moment.'

Kiril's usual sophistication had deserted him. He moved nearer, slipping an arm around her shoulders, turning her to face him. She gave a slight movement of protest, but Kiril's grip tightened. His eyes held hers until he felt he was drowning in their sea-green depths. His prepared speech was forgotten. He said hoarsely: 'Marry me, Eleanor.'

She gasped, her hand flying to her throat.

He drew her nearer. 'I see I have taken you by surprise, but you must know that I love you.'

'But I couldn't . . . You know nothing about me.' Not even my real name, she thought wildly.

'I know enough,' the Prince said confidently. And

before she could protest he bent his head to hers, kissing her full on the lips. His kiss was pleasant and firm, his arms strong and tender. Catherine felt a gentle response and when he lifted his head, his eyes were triumphant. He had aroused no passion in her yet, but he would teach her. He would have all the time in the world to teach her.

'So the answer is yes?'

'No,' Catherine shook her head against his shoulder, still imprisoned in his arms.

He frowned. 'I know you feel some affection for me, Eleanor. I can tell by the feel of your lips, by the way we laugh and talk together. I can offer you far more than any other man can. A title; vast wealth. We have no need to live in Russia. A country estate in England: a villa on the Riviera: anything you desire can be yours. Yurovsky would bore you in ten days. Count Leon Sukhanov is a fool. Lixy is too young to know his own mind.'

Desperately Kiril thought of any other rivals he could dispose of. 'Dominic is to marry Amelia Cunningham. Who else is there who could offer you what I can, or love you as I do?'

Catherine was barely aware of who Yurovsky or Sukhanov were, Lixy's name passed without a second thought. But that Dominic was to marry Amelia Cunningham ran through her head so that she had to press her fingers to her temples. There was no more hope. She could not return to London—not after the disgraceful manner of her leaving. She doubted if her step-mother would allow her to cross the threshold. All the future held was exile with her grandmother in Paris.

Kiril's hair waved smoothly back from a well-shaped

forehead. The blue eyes were pleading; the pressure of his lips had been warm and comforting. He was offering her not only wealth and a title, but love.

'Marry me, Eleanor,' he repeated, tilting her chin upwards with his index finger. 'Marry me, my darling, and I promise I will love you for eternity.'

Catherine stared unseeingly at the swans, the words strangled in her throat. 'I can't, Kiril. Not yet. There's so much about me that you do not know. When you do, you may feel differently.'

'Impossible.' He bent his head, kissing her with fervour. 'I want no confessions now. Nothing to mar the happiness of this moment.'

'But I haven't said yes,' Catherine protested.

'Yes you have, my darling, whether you realise it or not. I take it my grandmother knows all about the mystery in your past that you feel, so foolishly, could change my affections for you?'

'Of course,' Catherine was shocked, 'she knows everything.'

'And she still thinks that you would make me an ideal wife. So you see you are worrying your pretty little head about nothing. Let's hurry back and tell her immediately.'

'No. Not yet.' Panic seized her. 'I must think about it a little longer, Kiril.'

He smiled, sure of her. 'Our engagement will be announced on my grandmother's name day. That's in just over a week. Think about it as much as you like, my darling. Your answer is yes and in a week's time the whole world will know.' And feeling like a conquering hero he led her back towards the palace.

There would be loose ends to tidy up. His little opera singer would be distressed, but he was a Russian and even at the moment of proposing marriage to a woman he desperately desired, Kiril did not envisage a lifetime of fidelity. To do so would be to flout the laws of nature. All a man needed was discretion and he could always have the best of both worlds. He would have a wife the envy of every other man he met, and if certain other ladies required a little tenderness now and again, well then; he was man enough to supply it. He smiled happily to himself as he strolled across the sun-dappled lawns, Catherine's hand tucked in his arm.

There was a hum of excitement as they entered the palace. From the white-gold salon came the chatter of voices, and as they entered, Catherine was surprised to see that even Maria had been carried from her own salon to lie on the Princess's rose-silk chaise-longue.

'Do you really think there will be a war?' she was asking Lixy, her gentle face apprehensive.

'There's bound to be,' Lixy replied optimistically. 'It's been in the air ever since the Arch-Duke was shot.'

Through the open window came the sound of screaming brakes and a cloud of dust rose as the Panhard swerved to a halt at the main entrance and Alexis hurried from the car, running into the palace without even waiting for the strip of red carpet to be unrolled.

'Whatever can be the matter with Alexis?' Maria asked. 'Do you think he has news? Oh I *do* so hope it isn't war! I couldn't bear it!'

Seen only by Catherine, Dominic followed Alexis at a leisurely pace, his face grave. At the very sight of him her stomach turned a dizzy somersault and she clenched her hands in her lap, saying mentally over and over again 'He's going to marry Amelia Cunningham, he's going to marry Amelia Cunningham.' And then, more spiritedly, 'If he shows *so* little taste, what can I possibly see in him? *And* he's rude and insulting. Kiril would never treat any woman in the way Dominic treated me. Not even if he did think her a lady of the streets.' But as he came into the salon, her knees weakened and she had to turn her head away, unable to look at him and hold onto her anger at the same time.

'War!' Alexis roared, charging across the salon, precious Wedgwood and Meissen teetering precariously.

Maria's face was ashen. 'I don't believe it! It's too hideous to be true!'

'It's true,' Alexis was exhilarated. 'The Tsar met the President of France days ago. I told you I spoke to him at the official banquet. He said then it would be declared within a month and he was right.'

'We're living through fateful days!' the Baroness said, clasping her hands ecstatically. 'Everyone knows it. Historic days! My brother in Paris has sent me a little box with some Lorraine soil in it. We will soon have Alsace and Lorraine belonging to France again and those nasty old Germans taught a lesson!'

'Don't spill soil over *my* carpets,' the Princess said grimly, 'Lorraine or otherwise.'

'The French President reviewed the troops,' Alexis said enthusiastically. 'Over sixty thousand men and all of them ready to fight!'

'There will be nothing left of Austria,' the Baroness said happily. 'Nothing at all!'

'And what has Austria done to you?' the Princess

asked crushingly. 'You really are a fool, Lena.'

Lena shook her head, a curl disentangling itself and spiralling down over one ear. 'If I am a fool, so is everyone else, Dagmar. Everyone wants war.' Catherine shivered. Like Maria, the thought of war was abhorrent to her.

'If there is going to be a war it's not going to interfere with my name day,' the Princess said resolutely.

'Have the invitations gone out yet, Lena?'

'A ball?' Kiril asked incredulously. 'We can't have a ball now!'

'Why not? We've had a ball on my name day for the past seventy years. I see no reason to change the habit of a lifetime because of a passing excitement in the Balkans.

'If we invite all the Embassy staff we will get all the latest news. Together with the Cunninghams that will be enough. No disrespect Eleanor, but I don't want to be over-run with Britons. Life is grim enough as it is.'

The next few days were a hectic rush. There was the ball to prepare for and also a formal banquet to attend with the Tsar and Tsarina in attendance. Catherine wore the emerald tiara and necklace, while the Princess was resplendent in a breathtaking display of diamonds. For the first time Catherine saw the Tsarina and was startled to see the lines of suffering on the still beautiful face.

Two days later she accompanied the Princess and Kiril to the review of troops. It was blisteringly hot and the Princess complained volubly throughout, threatening to leave for the Crimea the minute the review was over. Kiril never left Catherine's side, pointing out name after name of Russian nobility, impatient to be able to

announce to them that Eleanor was to be his wife. A vast
army of white picture-hats and parasols turned simul-
taneously as the Imperial party arrived, the Tsar galloping by the side of the Tsarina's carriage, followed by a
brilliant escort of Grand Dukes and aides.

'Pretty girls,' the Princess said gruffly at the sight of
the two elder Grand Duchesses in a carriage with their
mother. 'This is what the people want. Spectacle and
pageantry.'

At the end of the afternoon, as the sun dipped in a
blaze of flame, the Tsar gave the signal for the evening
prayer. Thousands and thousands of people uncovered
their heads as the band played a hymn and the Pater was
recited in a loud voice. In that moment of stillness, as the
people prayed for the Tsar and for Russia, Catherine felt
her throat tighten and saw the Princess reach for a
handkerchief and hastily dab at her eyes. 'Magnificent,'
the Baroness said reverently. 'Magnificent. Did you ever
see such fighting men? What chance Germany now!'

At the palace scores of rooms were opened and aired
for overnight guests, the beds made up with fine linen
sheets embroidered with the Princess's initials and family coat-of-arms. The footmen spent hours polishing the
ballroom floor, skating across it with large dusters tied to
their feet till the surface shone like glass. The gardeners
planted hydrangeas around the balconies, transporting
barrow loads of plants into the ballroom itself so that it
resembled an indoor garden. Kiril was still determined
to announce their engagement on the evening of the
ball, and as every day passed Catherine was still no
nearer a decision.

She was sitting by the goldfish pool, her hand trailing

in the water as she tried to decide what to do. Quick footsteps sounded in the distance and she turned her head, catching her breath as Dominic strode towards her. It was the first time he had paid her any attention in weeks. As he drew nearer she felt her heart begin to beat in slow, thick strokes and she had an irresistible urge to run away.

He looked down at her, his eyes inscrutable. 'I am going into Petersburg to catch the excitement. Would you like to join me?'

It was the first time he had ever requested her company. She knew that she should refuse, but found herself asking weakly,

'What excitement?'

'A declaration of war is imminent and I want to be there when it is announced.' He paused, a suspicious quirk at the corner of his mouth. 'Perhaps you would prefer to walk the streets of St Petersburg alone?'

'That remark is quite unjustified,' Catherine said, springing to her feet, her eyes hot with scalding tears.

'It is,' he said gravely. 'I have it on very good authority from Princess Dagmar that your reputation is above reproach.'

'I presume that without the Princess's reference you would not deign to be seen with me in public,' Catherine retorted, angry sparks flashing in her eyes.

'Of course not.' His voice was smooth but she knew he was laughing at her. 'But as I *did* rescue you from a fate worse than death, the least you can do is to be courteous enough to accompany me.'

'I assume Amelia Cunningham is otherwise engaged at the moment,' Catherine said icily.

'Regretfully so.'

Despite her anger she felt her nerves begin to throb as his eyes held hers unflinchingly.

'Are you coming or not? The war will be announced, fought and over if we debate the subject any longer.'

'Yes,' Catherine said, despising herself for her weakness and cursing herself for a fool. 'After all,' she smiled sweetly, 'a war isn't declared every day and sacrifices must be made.'

'The sacrifice being my company?' A cynical eyebrow rose quizzically.

Catherine did not deign to reply. There was a slight frown on his face as he stared down at her and then he escorted her to where the Vishnetski landau waited.

'Are you always so uncommunicative?' he asked, his body so near to hers that she could feel its heat, the strength of his thigh muscles as he walked closely at her side. 'It's unbecoming in a red-head.'

'My hair isn't red: it's titian,' Catherine snapped, wishing he would not hold her arm in such intimate closeness.

He stopped walking and turned her round slowly, standing very close to her so that she could feel his breath upon her cheek. The expression in his eyes as he gazed down at her made her heart race.

'It's red,' he said and this time there was no mockery in his eyes, 'and very beautiful.' He reached out a hand and touched her face tenderly. She turned away from him and said, in a strangled voice.

'Is war *really* going to be declared?'

'Any minute. The streets are full of expectant crowds. Why do you always so persistently change the subject? I tell you your hair is beautiful and you ask me about war.'

'If I took every word you have said to me at its face value, I would have had grounds for slander,' Catherine said tartly, recovering her equilibrium with difficulty.

He laughed, and his face no longer looked harsh or forbidding. 'Surely I have made apologies enough? After all, it was late and it was dark and under the circumstances . . .'

'I am well aware of what you thought in the circumstances and have no desire to discuss the subject further.'

'I see I still have to make amends,' he said, his grasp firm as he handed her into the landau.

She sat opposite him stiffly, her eyes avoiding his.

The minute they left the Vishnetski estate and headed towards the bridge they could hear the roar of the distant crowds. Scores of hurrying people massed the road, heading for the centre of the city.

'Is it war?' Dominic shouted to a man clutching a pile of broadsheets.

'Yes, thank God!' came the reply and he thrust a smudged black-printed paper into Dominic's outstretched hand.

The Imperial double eagle headed the page and at the foot was the signature of the Minister of War.

'I can't believe it,' Catherine said aghast. 'Is Britain at war too? Shouldn't we go back and tell the Princess and Maria?'

'They will learn soon enough. Let's follow the crowd to the Winter Palace. This is history, Eleanor, and we are going to be part of it.'

The restraint between them ebbed away as they were

caught up in the excitement of the crowds running alongside their carriage.

As they neared the Neva the crowds were so dense that the landau was hemmed in, rocking perilously.

'Take the carriage back to the palace,' Dominic shouted to the coachman. Then, with a grin that transformed his handsome face, 'We'll go the rest of the way on foot!'

He sprang from the carriage, putting both hands round her waist to swing her to the ground. In that split second, with his face so close to hers, the sun burnishing his black curls to shining jet, the full mobile mouth laughing up at her, Catherine felt her whole being respond. She put her arms around his neck, feeling as carefree as the cheering crowds who surrounded them, not objecting as he seized her hand and they joined the swarming mass, jostling its way towards the Winter Palace.

Through the noise and confusion the bells of Kazan Cathedral began to boom and then the mellower bells of St Isaac's, the bells of the Nevsky Monastery. Total strangers shouted greetings, shaking hands vigorously, slapping backs. Paper streamers were thrown from windows and alleys and in small squares full-scale parties were in progress.

'To the Palace Square!' a man cried, holding a young child by its hand. 'The Tsar is coming! To the Palace Square!'

Jammed in a jubilant crowd, Dominic's arm protectively round her, they laughed and gasped their way down to the quay.

The sun burned down relentlessly on their heads,

Catherine's parasol long since lost in the crush. On the glittering sheet of water, a mass of yachts and skiffs, sailboats and rowing boats waited in a fever of excitement for the arrival of the Tsar from Peterhof. Flags streamed from masts, the decks were crammed with sweltering spectators, the bridges and quays a teeming mass of singing, cheering humanity. Then there was such a roar that the very ground seemed to shake.

'Is that the Tsar?' Catherine gasped, crushed to Dominic's chest. 'Oh, I can't see!'

He grinned and lifted her bodily off her feet and over the heads of the crowd Catherine could see the Tsar and Tsarina leave their yacht and step onto the quay at the Palace Bridge. Banners were unfurled, icons waved and cheer after cheer rolled over the small figure in army uniform and the straight-backed woman in a gleaming white dress. A crush of people burst forward, frantically trying to touch the Tsar's hand and kiss his feet.

'We need to get to the front of the Palace,' Dominic shouted to her. 'He'll be making a speech. Hold tight!'

All of Russia had the same idea. Forcefully Dominic shouldered his way through the crowd, holding Catherine tightly by the hand, shielding her with his body when the crush threatened to swamp her entirely. High above them the balcony had been draped in red velvet and as far as the eye could see a cheering crowd surged and swayed. Then, just as Catherine thought she could stand on her feet no longer, the Tsar appeared on the balcony and she was submerged in noise. Roar after roar rolled over the giant square, echoing from the glittering walls of the Palace, across the Neva, spreading like wildfire the length and breadth of Russia.

Overcome with emotion the Tsar bowed his head and the crowd stumbled to its knees, fervently singing the Imperial Anthem.

They sang with such faith and hope that tears came to Catherine's eyes. Russia was at war and Russia would win. It was an exhilarating thought. Dominic's arm tightened round her so that she could feel the strong, steady beat of his heart next to hers. She raised her face to his, and in the centre of Palace Square, surrounded by hundreds and thousands of cheering Russians, he bent his head to hers and kissed her, long and lingeringly.

This time he did not swing on his heel and leave her. Her lips parted softly beneath his, her arms crept shyly round his neck. Slowly he raised his head, their eyes holding. They could have been on a desert island instead of in the centre of one of the largest crowds Europe had ever seen. She was held so close to his chest that she could feel the heavy slam of his heart.

'I don't know what I am going to do about you,' he said, his voice thick and strangely unsteady, and then, when she clung to him weakly, he bent his head and kissed her again with burning ferocity.

Catherine could no more have restrained herself from responding than ceased to breathe.

He wound his fingers in her hair so that the careful hairstyle Vilya had created came tumbling down around her shoulders.

'I have been every kind of a fool, Eleanor. Will you forgive me?' he asked with a depth of feeling in his voice that startled her.

'You thought I was a fallen woman,' she said shakily.

Something hot flickered at the back of his eyes. 'Then the least I could have done was reclaim you.' His arms circled her shoulders. 'Let's get out of this crush before we suffocate.'

The sun beat down mercilessly as they struggled through the sweltering crowd, dazzling their eyes as they finally squeezed out of the worst of the crush, leaning weakly against the walls of the Cathedral.

'I feel as if I have been in a war myself,' Catherine said, trying to neaten her crumpled dress and dishevelled hair, her hand trembling violently.

He lifted a tendril of hair away from her face. 'You look very beautiful.'

Kiril told her that a hundred times a day. It had never sent shivers down her spine or made it difficult for her to breathe.

'We need to talk,' he said, the warmth of his touch spreading through her like fire.

Hand in hand they made their way between jubilant groups of soldiers to the cool serenity of the English church.

Stepping across the threshold was like stepping into another world. Instead of incense there was the familiar smell of polished wood. Instead of icons and statues, the quiet dignity of Anglicanism. They could have been in any church in any English village. The organ played a familiar hymn. She reached for a hymn book. The pews in front were filled with elderly ladies in a variety of splendid hats. Here and there a young head bowed decorously, neat buns signifying a governess. Bowing to events, the next hymn was slightly more marching and military, but that was the only concession the English church was making to the outbreak of Russia's war with Germany.

As the service finished she rose to her feet, and he laid a hand on her arm, restraining her. At that moment the imposing figure of Lady Cunningham bore down upon them. Catherine's joy vanished. This was reality. Lady Cunningham. Amelia's mother. Dominic's future mother-in-law.

'My dear Marquis,' Lady Cunningham exclaimed in a loud, carrying voice. 'What a delightful surprise.' Her heavy eyebrows rose at the sight of Catherine. She tilted her pince-nez to her eyes so that she could assure herself that she had not made a mistake.

Well aware of the hawk-like gaze Catherine met it defiantly. With raised eyebrows Lady Cunningham transferred her attentions back to the Marquis.

'I suppose this announcement of war means an exodus from Petersburg before the frontiers close?'

'Perhaps.' Dominic's tone was non-committal, his hand still firmly beneath Catherine's elbow.

'It would be pleasanter to leave together,' she continued, ignoring Catherine as if she did not exist.

'My plans are rather flexible at the moment,' Dominic said with a cool smile. 'Good day,' and holding Catherine's arm in a vice-like grip he led her out of the dimmed church into the blinding sunshine.

'She is furious with you,' Catherine said bleakly.

A broad shoulder gave a slight shrug.

'She *is* to be your mother-in-law. Don't you mind?'

He stopped so abruptly that she nearly fell, swinging her round to face him. 'I would mind like hell if she were! Who filled your head with that nonsense?'

'Kiril.' Catherine felt herself sway. He wasn't going to marry Amelia. Kiril had been wrong. The heat; the violent swing from ecstasy to misery and back to ecstasy again, was too much for her. With a little cry she felt her knees give way as rushing darkness pressed in on her and she sank into oblivion.

CHAPTER
EIGHT

WHEN she regained consciousness it was to find herself being carried bodily in strong arms, pressed close against the hardness of a strongly muscled chest. Her eyes flickered open and he looked down at her, as he said,

'I shall probably have to carry you all the way back to Verechenko. There won't be a droshky to be found today.'

Catherine suppressed a smile. The expression in his eyes was one she had longed to see: one of tenderness. Her arms tightened around his neck. She knew her happiness could be short-lived. Soon she must tell him who she was, and she had no way of knowing what Dominic's reaction would be, but for the moment the afternoon was theirs and Catherine wanted it to last for ever.

'I am feeling much better now,' she said. 'Let's not go back to Verechenko yet. There's too much happening in Petersburg.'

This time there was no mistaking the anxiety in the dark eyes. 'Are you sure?'

'Quite sure.'

He showed as little inclination to set her back down on her feet as Catherine felt to be set down. Carrying her as though she were no more than a feather, he strode

145

through the excited crowd, the populace instinctively recognising one of the nobility and making way for him.

St Petersburg was *en fête*, the whole city one incredible gay party. He smiled down at her. A smile that made her heart turn over. 'Then we'll do it in at least some semblance of comfort.'

Only a man of Dominic's distinctive bearing could have managed to get a droshky on a day when the entire city filled the streets. Head and shoulders above the crowd, a brief nod of the dark head was enough to have a droshky driver force his way towards them, ignoring all other demands for his services. Gently he set her down on a seat, hard after the luxury of the Vishnetski and Dolgorovsky carriages.

Catherine was unaware of any discomfort. Dominic's hand still held hers. The harshness that in repose gave his handsome face such a forbidding appearance had gone; as had the bleak unhappiness that clouded his eyes when none could see. He was a man transformed. His eyes were alight with an expression that sent her heart racing. In a few, brief, magic-filled moments their whole relationship had changed and rejoicing filled her as it did the hundreds and thousands of flag-waving Russians who crowded the streets and squares.

Every turning revealed another party. Hands joined, held high, neighbours danced in huge, boisterous circles, overjoyed at the prospect of an overwhelming victory for their country.

What the war would mean to her, Catherine neither knew nor cared. Before the day was over she would have told Dominic the truth and her future would be determined. For Catherine, love dominated over war. Only when her heart was secure would she be able to take in the full implications of what the celebrations around her signified.

Dominic knew only too well what it signified and he knew it was no cause for the rejoicing going on around him. He also knew that he had to talk to the maddening, exasperating, beautiful and unpredictable girl he had fallen in love with. And like Catherine, but for different reasons, he dreaded it. He knew, too, that this golden afternoon could well be the only hours of happiness they would spend together, for he had no way of knowing what her reaction would be when he spoke to her. Paper streamers showered into the droshky and Dominic laughed, throwing them back at the crowd, banishing dark thoughts, savouring the precious time they had together. As the afternoon faded into evening, Catherine rested her head happily on his shoulder, the droshky driver, overwhelmed at the number of roubles Dominic had dropped into his hand, driving them slowly back across the Neva to Verechenko.

Dominic gently wound his fingers through her hair that hung waist length, the last of the restraining pins long since scattered on the St Petersburg streets. They tightened as he felt passion rising like a tide within him. Verechenko gleamed pearl-white in the distance. The idyll was almost at an end. His fingers knotted tightly in the gleaming gold hair as he kissed her urgently and hungrily, his longing for her almost unbearable.

The droshky driver coughed loudly. It was no affair of his how the aristocracy behaved, but he could recognise Princess Dagmar Dolgorova when he saw her, and the wizened figure on Verechenko's balcony was unmistakably that of Her Highness.

Abruptly Dominic let Catherine go, glancing intuitively upwards, his eyes meeting Princess Dagmar's. Catherine was too shocked by the violence of her own emotions to be aware of the Princess's presence. Hardly able to breathe, oblivious of anyone or anything, she allowed Dominic to escort her into Verechenko's marbled entrance hall.

'I must see Dagmar,' Dominic was saying, and all the things she had been going to say to him were left unsaid.

Unsteadily she climbed the wide sweep of staircase to her boudoir. Vilya gasped in horror at the sight of her mistress, hair swinging waist length like that of a peasant. Her pretty dress in such disorder that the hem was not only thick with dirt but torn into the bargain. And the expression on her face! Her eyes and cheeks were radiant, the full curving lips bruised as if by kisses, and she had not been out with Prince Kiril, that Vilya *did* know. She brushed the red-gold hair vigorously. Perhaps Dmitri would know where Miss Eleanor had been. One thing was for sure. Princess Dagmar would soon find out. Nothing happened in Verechenko without the Princess's knowledge.

Lena bustled into the room, a yapping Spaniel under one arm, a barking Pekinese under the other.

'Such excitement! Such activity! Kiril has been summoned to see the Minister of War. Naturally he will head a regiment. Oh, the glory he will bring to the family! And Dagmar is still going ahead with her name-day ball tomorrow evening. A double celebration!' She clapped her hands ecstatically. 'It will be wonderful. Men look so *handsome* in uniform, don't you think?'

The Baroness chatted on and Catherine wondered when she would be able to speak to Dominic. There could be no more deception between them. She would speak to him immediately after dinner.

The vast dinner table was set only for three. The Baroness still chattering ten to the dozen, the Princess, with a peculiar glint in her eyes, and Catherine.

'Where is everybody?' Catherine ventured at last.

'Kiril and Alexis are at the Ministry,' the Princess said, watching Catherine closely.

Kiril. Catherine had not given him the slightest thought all day. She would have to see him the minute he returned, tell him she had made her decision and that she was unable to marry him.

'And the Marquis,' she asked, her voice trembling slightly.

'He is at the British Embassy. He wants to know what your country's position is. Whether Britain will enter the war or not.'

'Britain?' It had never occurred to Catherine that Britain, so far away, could be involved with the events taking place in Russia.

'They have offered support,' the Baroness interrupted. 'Not that Russia needs support. We are strong enough to fight our own battles.'

Catherine felt suddenly cold. If Britain were to enter the war, Dominic would have to fight. What if anything should happen to him? The thought did not bear thinking about.

'You look pale, Eleanor,' the Princess said. 'Are you feeling all right?'

'Yes, thank you.'

Only in privacy did Dagmar refer to Catherine by her proper name. She signalled for her glass of wine to be re-filled, her eyes thoughtful. After dinner she dismissed Lena and Catherine with a tired wave of her hand.

'I am going to bed. The arrangements for tomorrow have tired me out,' she said, and she walked slowly out of the room accompanied only by her maid and little negro servant.

Catherine stared after her. It was the first time she had known the Princess admit to tiredness or to walk without her customary sprightliness.

Much as she liked Lena, she felt unable to endure an evening of enthusiasm about the war and Alsace and Lorraine. Instead she joined Maria, sitting with her as she had done before becoming Dagmar's companion, finding Maria's gentle company soothing. Several times she nearly confided in her and asked her advice, but each time the moment passed. What advice could Maria give her? She knew what she had to do. She waited impatiently for the sound of any arriving carriage or automobile, but none came. At eleven Maria's maid came to prepare her for bed and Catherine wandered restlessly back to her room. She would have to contain herself. Wait until tomorrow. She felt a surge of relief. If Dominic's reaction was what she feared, then she had been spared it a little while longer. She dismissed Vilya and climbed into bed, re-living again all the events of the day, with that last, passionate embrace that had evoked feelings in her so strong and disturbing that even in the darkness she felt her cheeks flush.

The next day was chaos as the servants made the final

preparations for the ball. The cooks and kitchen maids worked ceaselessly, preparing pastries and delicacies for the evening. Crate after crate of champagne was chilled. Strange carriages arrived, early visitors being shown to the prepared guest rooms and vast armies of maids scurried up and down corridors with armfuls of glittering dresses.

Endlessly the day wore on and still there was no sign of Dominic. The Princess and Lena disappeared to begin their toilettes and Vilya grew impatient, feeling herself personally responsible for Catherine's appearance that evening. At last, reluctantly, Catherine left the terrace where she had waited all day, and allowed Vilya to brush her hair into elaborate curls, decorated with diamond butterfly pins.

There was a soft tap on the door and Vilya draped Catherine's naked shoulders with a negligee before answering it. A footman stood there, a gold wrapped box in his hands.

Vilya took it, shutting the door quickly before the man could get more than a brief glimpse of the Princess's companion in nothing more than a confection of silk and lace, and handed the package to Catherine. Inside, lying on a bed of moss, lay a single, perfect rose. The petals were milk-white, velvet soft, the perfume heady and intoxicating. The card had simply Dominic's name scrawled across in powerful black lettering. With trembling hands she laid the rose back in its box, determined to wear no other ornamentation that evening. Her dress was of heavy sea-green satin, a colour matching exactly that of her eyes, the decolletage daringly low and edged with seed-pearls, hugging her breasts, the skirt falling

behind her in a small train. Vilya had brushed her hair
till it shone like fire, bringing out tray after tray of
jewellery for Catherine to choose from.

'No thank you, Vilya,' Catherine said. 'I shall wear
only my rose.'

Vilya stared at her appalled. 'No jewellery? But you
must wear jewellery. The emerald tiara and necklace?
Or the rubies? Or perhaps even just pearls?' Her voice
faltered as she saw the determination in Catherine's
eyes.

Catherine smiled at her. 'No Vilya, only my rose.'

As Vilya saw her mistress in the full-length triple
mirrors she ceased to protest. Catherine's judgment was
faultless. The colour of the dress showed off the fiery
nebula of her hair to perfection. The low bodice revealed perfect breasts and Vilya doubted if there would
be another woman in the ballroom with a waist as small.
Catherine had removed the carefully placed diamond
butterfly pins from her hair and Vilya pinned the rose in
their place. With not a jewel on her, Catherine's youth
and beauty would stand out from the other guests like
that of an exquisite dove amongst a bevy of poppinjays.

Dominic would surely be downstairs at the ball. With
her throat tight and her mouth dry, Catherine allowed
Vilya to spray her with perfume and prepared to join the
Princess.

The Princess had forsaken the heavy ropes of pearls
she loved so much and was wearing a breathtaking collar
of emeralds, her silver-grey dress shimmering with a
hundred thousand brilliants. The plucked eyebrows rose
as Catherine entered the room. All those necklaces,
pendants, bracelets from Fabergé, the tiara specially

made for this evening, all were missing. Even, the Princess noted quickly, the sapphire ring. Nothing but a white rose nestling in her hair. Did the girl know the ravishing effect she had created?

'Sometimes,' she said to Catherine, 'I don't know whether you are a very simple girl or a very clever one,' and she swept from her boudoir leaving Catherine mystified. Standing regally at the head of the magnificent staircase, the Princess greeted her guests, flanked by Catherine and Lena. It was as both Vilya and the Princess had known it would be. Not a man bowing over Princess Dagmar's hand and kissing it, could keep his eyes from Catherine. Yet she seemed totally unaware of the reaction she was causing.

The Princesses and Countesses, the Baronesses and Duchesses, carefully avoided giving Catherine even the merest acknowledgement. Not because they believed her to be socially inferior, though certainly Lady Cunningham had made sure that the English community were aware of the fact, but out of seething anger at the besottedness of their menfolk. Suddenly the costly stones that graced their throats and ears seemed garishly commonplace. To outdo another woman in the extravagance of jewels in St Petersburg was an impossibility. Princess Dagmar's companion's decision to wear only a rose was, in the eyes of the ladies, a masterstroke. Even the representative from the British Embassy, a distinguished-looking gentleman by the name of William Townley, gazed admiringly at her. He knew of course, that according to Lady Cunningham the girl was nothing but a governess that the eccentric Princess had decided to foist upon polite society. Mr Townley, a mature

gentleman in his fifties, was sure she was wrong. He
knew a lady when he saw one and he was certain he was
seeing one now. Lena fidgeted with her fan nervously.
The Englishman was very attractive, with his steel-grey
hair and quiet manner. Perhaps later he would dance
with her. The thought made her so apprehensive she
dropped the fan altogether and William Townley cour-
teously retrieved it, handing it to her with a bow and
smile that flustered her even further.

The envy in the eyes of the Russian ladies was nothing
to the expression in the eyes of Lady Cunningham and
Amelia.

Amelia had dressed with great care, certain that
tonight was the night that the Marquis would propose to
her. She had chosen to wear a diaphanous gown of white
chiffon in the hope that it would make him realise how
utterly breathtaking she would look in her wedding
gown. Diamonds sparkled in her blonde hair, caressed
her throat and clung in wide bracelets around her arms.
Lady Cunningham's own drop earrings of priceless diamonds hung from her tiny ears nearly to her shoulders.

She would be queen of the ball and it was in this
confident expectation that she entered the ballroom. A
few heads turned, but not many. Certainly she had not
heard the concerted inward gasp of admiration, that her
entrance, decked in diamonds from head to foot, would
have caused in London. Beneath the lights of a hundred
chandeliers, every other woman present was wearing a
king's ransom of jewellery.

And then Amelia saw Catherine. She would have had
to be blind to be unaware that the eyes of every man in
the room were rivetted on her rival. Her little cat-like

eyes closed to mere slits. She would make quite sure that
the Marquis was under no misapprehension about
Eleanor's background. That her mother had informed
him on numerous occasions and without seeming effect,
Amelia knew. But this time *she* would tell him. That
Eleanor was invited to the ball at all was an insult to
herself and to her mother.

The Princess, the reception complete, entered the
ballroom, Catherine at her side.

Within seconds Lixy had foiled every other gentleman
present and asked her for the first waltz. Lightly in Lixy's
arms she danced round and around, the vast ballroom a
fairyland of colour and light, but of the face she was
searching for there was no sign.

'I suppose you know you are creating a sensation,'
Lixy said, his eyes admiring.

'Me?' she looked at him in genuine surprise.

Lixy laughed. It was going to be pleasant hav-
ing Eleanor's continued company, for he knew that
Kiril intended marrying her. Some wives could make
friendships between men difficult. This one wouldn't.
He enjoyed her company just as much as he did
Kiril's.

'At this rate we'll never get her back as governess,'
Alexis said glumly to Maria, whose chaise-longue had
been brought down into the ballroom.

Maria laughed, clasping her husband's hand. 'I am
afraid you are right, darling. We must look elsewhere.
You know that Kiril intends marrying her?'

'Does he, by God!' Alexis, immune to any of the
undercurrents around him had known no such thing.
'When Dagmar realises that all hell will be let loose!'

'No it won't,' his wife chided. 'Dagmar has positively encouraged him to propose.'

Alexis' bushy eyebrows rose in disbelief. 'But she's a governess, Maria. Dagmar is mad, but she's not certifiable.'

Maria tapped him reprovingly with her fan. 'I've a feeling Dagmar knows more about Eleanor than we suspect. Look! Eleanor is dancing with Prince Yurovsky now and he looks absolutely smitten. Where is Kiril?'

'Doing his best to get away from the Minister. A ball the day after war has been declared isn't exactly convenient. You note no Government Ministers are present?'

'But he'll be here soon?'

'I should think he's champing at the bit to get away. He would be if he could see the way Yurovsky is flirting with Eleanor. Damn it all, the man looks as if he's going to propose himself any minute.'

'I think he already has,' Maria said smugly.

'And she turned him down? A prince!' Alexis exclaimed disbelievingly.

'I don't *know* that he has. Just my feminine intuition, and yet if he had or if he did then Eleanor would turn him down.'

'Feminine intuition again?'

'Yes, dear.'

'I don't know how you do it.'

'No dear, I know you don't.' Her big, kind Alexis hadn't one ounce of intuition. 'Why don't you dance with Eleanor when this dance finishes? She looks as though she desperately wants to escape from Prince Yurovsky's clutches. You can't stand beside me *all* the evening.'

'Why not? I enjoy it. You're beautiful. In fact, you're so beautiful I've a good mind to kiss you.'

'Not in front of all of St Petersburg society,' Maria said giggling. '*Especially* your wife! How ridiculous you are, Alexis. Now, the music is finishing, off you go.'

With an exaggerated sigh of obedience, Alexis made his way towards Catherine. Balls and parties were not for him. He much preferred the wide-open spaces and the company of other men.

Prince Yurovsky was brushed to one side with very little ceremony as Alexis swept Catherine away from under his nose.

'A pity the Countess is crippled,' Lady Cunningham said slyly to Lena, her face mottled with rage at the success Catherine was having, knowing full well that her own daughter was being put in the shade. She followed Alexis and Catherine around the room with a hard glint in her eye. 'It leaves a man so vulnerable, don't you think?'

'Oh, the Vishnetskis are terribly happy,' Lena said, wondering where William Townley had disappeared to and not for one moment grasping Lady Cunningham's insinuations.

'Maybe so,' Lady Cunningham continued undeterred, 'but I think Countess Vishnetskaya is nursing a viper in her bosom.'

'A what?' Anxiously Lena gazed across at Maria's decolletage.

'A viper,' Lady Cunningham repeated, thinking the Baroness an uncomprehending idiot. 'The way that hussy has ingratiated herself. After all, my dear Baroness, although Miss Cartwright is now acting as Princess

Dagmar's companion and indeed behaving as if she was one of the family, she *was* engaged as the Vishnetskis' governess, was she not?'

'Oh, but that was only a temporary arrangement,' Lena said kindly, she hd never bothered her head about who or what Eleanor was. She was a dear, sweet girl and that was all that mattered. 'In fact,' she leaned confidingly towards Lady Cunningham, 'I believe that she is going to marry the Prince.'

'The Prince!' Lady Cunningham's words were strangled in her throat. Her voice rose perilously high. 'What Prince?'

'Why, Kiril of course. They will make *such* a handsome couple.'

Lady Cunningham blanched. If what this blabbing fool was telling her was true, then her behaviour towards that wretched girl could well prove embarrassing. Innuendoes about a governess were one thing, about a princess quite another. And if she were to marry into the Dolgorovsky family then she *must* have breeding. Why, the Russians were stricter about such matters than the English. Lady Cunningham had the uncomfortable feeling that she had made a grave error of judgment.

As Alexis thanked Catherine formally for the dance, a Grand Duke immediately took his place, and then Baron von Bezabrov, Lixy again and then a General with so many medals on his chest that Catherine's bosom hurt. The Englishman William Townley danced with her, asking her about Baroness Kerenskaya and what relation she was to Princess Dagmar. Lixy danced with her again and then an officer from the Chevalier guards.

Her eyes scanned the shifting mass of dancing couples

in vain. Lena, slightly breathless, danced past in the arms of an elderly general. Countess Nestoreva was talking to a white-haired gentleman who looked unmistakably English. The dancers surged and swung, and then she saw him.

He was dancing with Amelia Cunningham and she was looking up at him in a way that made Catherine feel faint. Lixy brushed past her, a slim brunette in his arms. The music stopped. The guards officer retreated, her glass of champagne was replenished as she stood with Maria and Alexis, waiting desperately for Dominic to move towards her. The young guards officer came towards her again, smiling. The music began and she accepted his hand, waltzing off into the centre of the ballroom. Amelia drifted past, this time in the arms of the elderly Count Nestorev.

Then, as the dancers swung apart, Dominic's eyes met hers. The dark eyebrows rose, the near black eyes gleamed, and Catherine's heart hammered wildly against the crimson jacket of her partner. As the dance ended Dominic strode across to her so impatiently that heads turned.

'What do you mean by dancing with other men? I've been looking for you for hours.'

'You've only just arrived.' She risked a look into his eyes and her heart turned over. 'Besides, I saw you dancing with Amelia Cunningham only a moment ago.'

'Merely carrying out my duties,' he said dryly. The music had started up again. He swept her away, holding her close. 'So you would rather be with a young guards officer than with me?'

'No. I would rather be with you.'

'Good,' the strong arms around her tightened. The musicians swept past. She caught a glimpse of the Princess dancing with a military gentleman, Amelia's malicious eyes met hers and vanished.

'I missed you this afternoon,' she said shyly.

'I missed you too. I had forgotten you were so beautiful.'

Her heart beat up into her throat. They were at the far end of the ballroom and without missing a step Dominic waltzed her past a couple of elderly ladies sipping champagne and across the corridor into the deserted gold and white drawing room. The strains of the music followed them, softly muted. They danced round and round, a world apart from the hundreds of guests only yards away. The music died away and he held her in the centre of the candle-lit room, so close to his heart that she could hear it beating. Then, silently, he bent his head to hers and neither of them spoke for a very long time.

In the shadow of the doorway a squat figure watched them. Then, the expression on her face triumphant, Olga waddled quietly away. She had never forgiven Catherine for replacing her in the children's affections. Now she would have her revenge.

CHAPTER
NINE

AT LAST she said shakily: 'The Princess will be looking for me.'

'Damn the Princess.'

The strains of a mazurka filled the room as he kissed her again. Catherine felt as if she were on fire as he lowered his head, kissing her throat, her naked shoulder, the roundness of her breasts.

'Marry me,' he said huskily. 'For God's sake marry me and put me out of this torment.'

'Oh, yes,' Catherine felt tears of happiness spring to her eyes as she trembled beneath his touch, 'Oh yes, I will!'

Gently he lifted her face to his. 'And now we must talk.' She opened her mouth to speak, but he silenced it with a touch of his fingers. 'Sssh, my sweet love. There are things about me that you do not know. You may change your mind.'

'Never,' Catherine said vehemently. 'You see . . .'

This time he silenced her with a kiss. The room was too dark for her to see the gleam in his eyes as his arms circled her waist and he said: 'As the Marquis of Clare I must return to London and my family estates. I have to tell you this, my love, because I left under rather . . . difficult . . . circumstances . . .'

'Oh Dominic, please!' Catherine could contain herself no longer. 'It wasn't your fault!'

'But it was.' His voice changed, suddenly grave. 'I had an older brother whom I loved very much. He was tragically killed, murdered. I had been living in Paris for many years. I never met any woman I loved enough to ask to marry me. My father thought marriage would steady me, and as his heir I promised to give the matter some thought.' He paused. Catherine's tears had long since turned to tears of misery. 'My brother's fiancée was a young lady in difficult circumstances. Her father was on the verge of bankruptcy. God alone knew what would happen to her with Robert dead, so I offered to marry her myself.' He paused again and it was so still that Catherine could hear his pulse beating in the wrists that held her. 'Unfortunately my future mother-in-law was not a lady of discretion. She published the news far and wide even before there was an official announcement. Even before I had had the pleasure of meeting my future bride.'

He paused, and Catherine could feel her heart hammering wildly.

'The young lady in question took exception to my offer, did not deign to meet me and fled from London to her grandmother's, pronouncing me a dissolute woman-iser whom no decent girl would ever marry.' There was something very much like amusement in his voice. 'So you see what you would be getting, my love. The whole of London knew of the offer and will think you a young woman of very little taste in choosing to marry me.'

'Oh Dominic,' Catherine's voice was anguished. 'Oh

Dominic, *please* let me talk to you. *Please* let me explain . . .'

There came the sound of marching feet and Kiril burst into the room, white-faced and trembling.

'My God, Clare! I'll kill you for this!'

A score of servants ran hastily down the sides of the drawing room, lighting the chandeliers, and from the open doorway beyond Kiril the dancers in the ballroom looked across with interest. The music had changed to a slow waltz and even above the band and the laughter and conversation Kiril's words rang clearly.

'For what?' Dominic asked quietly, a dangerous light in his eyes.

'For luring my fiancée into a compromising situation!'

'Your fiancée?' Dominic's voice was ice-cold and deadly.

By now several couples had gathered interestedly in the doorway. As if in a nightmare Catherine was aware of Lena's girlish gown of rose pink and the incongruous rosebuds in the frizzed hair.

'Our engagement is to be announced this evening,' Kiril said tightly, wishing to God he had a sword to run through the arrogant Englishman. 'Eleanor accepted my offer a week ago. I have no alternative but to ask you to leave Verechenko immediately.'

Dominic stared from Kiril to Catherine, white-faced. 'If what you say is true, nothing would give me greater pleasure.'

Catherine held her breath. She felt as if she were drowning, submerged beneath relentless waves.

'*Everyone* knows Eleanor is to marry Kiril,' Lena was saying chirpily. 'It really is too bad of you, behaving like this. Spoiling things for them in this way.'

'Believe me, I wouldn't spoil things for them for the world,' Dominic's voice was a whiplash.

He looked across at Catherine, his eyes frightening in their intensity. 'Is it true that Dolgorovsky intended announcing your betrothal this evening?'

'Yes. But . . .' The room was closing in on Catherine, the blood drumming in her ears.

'Then all I can say, madam, is that my first impression of you was accurate. You may be beautiful but you are also a harlot!'

The group at the door had turned into a crowd. They gasped in delighted horror as Kiril's fist shot out, knocking Dominic to the floor. Slowly Dominic rose to his feet, his eyes blazing as the crowd made way for Princess Dagmar.

'I would beat the hell out of you, Dolgorovsky, only she's not worth the effort,' he rasped. 'You're welcome to her.' And before Catherine could cry out in protest he strode from the room, shouldering his way savagely through the goggle-eyed spectators.

'Dominic!' Catherine's voice seemed to come from a vast distance as she ran after him. 'Dominic, wait. Wait! Let me explain! Wait! Oh, please wait!'

Princess Dagmar barred her way. 'Distress yourself no further about his disgraceful conduct,' she said in her carrying voice. 'You behaved with great presence of mind in sending for help.'

An imperious wave of the cane was enough to send her guests scurrying speculatively back into the ballroom.

The doors were closed behind the three of them: Kiril

breathing harshly, Catherine only half conscious and the Princess, her face impassive.

'You will continue to behave as if nothing had happened. Under the circumstances there will be no public announcement of marriage this evening.'

'But . . .' Kiril interrupted hotly.

'But nothing. You understand nothing and never have done. Catherine, I will see you in my boudoir when the guests have departed.'

It was the first time she had used Catherine's name in Kiril's presence. He was too angry even to notice.

'But I must go to him!' Catherine protested, distraught.

The Princess's eyes held hers, freezing her where she stood.

'You will do no such thing. It would be of no avail. You forget that I understand the situation perfectly. Go back into the ballroom with Kiril and behave as if nothing has happened.'

Even as the Princess was speaking, Catherine knew that she was right. She wouldn't even be able to find Dominic now, and she knew that the only person who could explain the situation to him was the Princess. She must leave it in her hands and do as she was told. A look of silent understanding passed between them. Then the Princess turned her attention to her grandson.

Now was not the time to tell him he had lost Catherine, for she knew her companion well enough to know that even if the Marquis never spoke to her again, Catherine would not marry Kiril now. Kiril still didn't understand. It had never occurred to him that Catherine had been in the darkened room and in Dominic's arms out of choice. He would soon recover from his broken heart, and present her with some lifeless but suitable Princess as his bride.

With her heart breaking, Catherine allowed Kiril to lead her back into the ballroom. The Princess's presence quenched any rumours or gossip. The music played and Kiril led her out into the centre of the floor.

'It is no use arguing with my grandmother tonight,' he said bitterly. 'Clare has ruined everything.'

Behind discreet fans word had passed amongst the dowagers present of the scene in the small drawing-room till at last it had reached Lady Cunningham. The Marquis! *Amelia's* Marquis! Compromised by that brazen harlot and now already packing his bags and leaving before he had proposed to Amelia! Her mottled face was white with rage. And there she was, dancing in the arms of Prince Dolgorovsky as if nothing had happened! Lady Cunningham had an intense desire to commit murder.

'I am not marrying you,' Catherine was saying. 'I never did say I would, Kiril. Only that I would think about it.'

His steps faltered. 'Because of Clare's behaviour? Because you think I would be hurt by gossip?' He laughed. 'You don't understand Russians yet, my darling. The whole thing will be forgotten in twenty-four hours. This is St Petersburg, not London.'

Catherine shook her head. 'No, it's not because of that. I don't love you Kiril. I couldn't possibly marry you.'

He stared at her incredulously.

'Is there someone else? You love someone else?'

She could hold back the tears no longer.

'Yes,' she said as the tears fell unrestrainedly down her face. 'I love Dominic and now he will never have anything to do with me again!'

For once Kiril came into his own. Already passing couples had noticed Catherine's tear-wet cheeks and he led her quickly off the dance floor and onto the deserted flower-filled balcony. He had lost her. He knew it with certainty. She had never said she loved him, never given him a promise to marry, but he had gone ahead with his plans, confidently assuming. And now the Englishman, the man she loved, thought her flighty and of no account. Yet Kiril knew differently. He could tell by the suffering in her eyes the depths of her feelings for the Marquis. Kiril would have been inhuman if he had not felt a pang of jealousy at the love Dominic had aroused in Catherine. He had destroyed her happiness with careless words, the least he could do was to try and make amends.

'I am sorry,' he said gently. 'I will speak to him and explain.'

'He will have left now,' Catherine said between sobs. 'He could be anywhere. He won't stay in Petersburg. Your grandmother made it quite clear that he was forcing unwelcome attentions on me in order to protect my reputation. I have ruined him in London and now in St Petersburg.'

Kiril did not understand a word about London and decided not to tax his strength by enquiring. To him it was simple. He would follow the Marquis. Explain that Eleanor had never agreed to marry him and that the wedding announcement had been a gross assumption.

Eleanor and the Marquis would then live happily ever after and he could console himself with his little opera singer. It was all perfectly simple.

There was no sense in forcing Eleanor to endure the ballroom a moment longer. Risking his grandmother's wrath he led her unprotestingly towards her boudoir and an astonished looking Vilya.

'I think your mistress needs a warm brandy,' he said to Vilya. 'Ring for one and see that she is disturbed no more this evening.'

Vilya, backstairs gossip not yet having reached her, bobbed a curtsey and promised she would do so, wondering what on earth had happened. She had the good sense not to question Catherine. Silently she helped her out of her dress and draped a negligee over her shoulders while she summoned a footman for the prescribed warm brandy.

Catherine stared weakly into the mirror. The rose lay in her hair, as fresh, as fragile as it had been only brief hours ago when she had placed it there so carefully and happily.

Feeling as if her heart would break, she plucked it from its bed of curls and, smelling the sweet fragrance, crushed it between her fingers, laying her head on her arms and crying unrestrainedly.

Kiril strode through the endless rooms towards the suite occupied by the Marquis. Dominic's personal valet was busy packing countless clothes into monogrammed trunks.

'Where is the Marquis?' Kiril asked abruptly.

The valet cleared his throat uncomfortably. 'His Lordship has left. He gave me instructions to pack his wardrobe and to await further instructions when the trunks were collected.'

Kiril cursed beneath his breath. It was Russians who were supposed to be hot-headed and impulsive, not the normally cool English, though Kiril had never for a moment classified Dominic in the same category as most of his countrymen. He had always found Dominic's presence disturbing. The women fluttered round him like moths around a flame, and he seemed impervious to them. Only Catherine had aroused him and Kiril could well understand why. Even as he called for his carriage, he wondered if he was slightly mad, going to all this trouble to reunite the woman he had wanted to marry with a man who had the audacity to refer to her as a harlot. And in public! Not for the first time did Kiril feel he would never understand women.

The music from the ballroom rose and fell. Gay laughter drifted down behind him as he ran, his valet hurriedly throwing an evening cloak around his shoulders as he stepped into the waiting carriage.

'To the Narymovna,' he said, leaning back against the padded leather as the stallions broke into a gallop down Verechenko's impressive driveway.

Whether Dominic was a frequenter of the notorious club Kiril had no way of knowing. He could only judge Dominic by himself. If he had felt himself to have been made a fool of over a woman, his immediate reaction would be to forget his humiliation in other arms. In fact, under the circumstances, Kiril wanted nothing more than to get the damned business of Dominic and Eleanor sorted out so that he could pursue his own pleasures in the Narymovna.

While there had been hope of marrying Eleanor he had behaved with great discretion, his desire for her overwhelming his desire for lesser women. Now, philosophically resigned to the fact that he would never possess her, his thoughts were already on the tempting lips and abandoned bodies of the Narymovna girls.

The St Petersburg streets, always a mass of seething gaiety late at night as carriages drew up depositing bare-shouldered women in glittering gowns, was so crowded this particular night that Kiril despaired of ever reaching his destination. For the first time he felt no elation at the coming war. Without it, half of the crowd would have nothing to celebrate and his carriage would be able to force its way through. As it was, even a carriage bearing the Dolgorovsky coat-of-arms was brought to a standstill time and time again by singing, drunken mobs. Kiril leant his head out of the window, crying 'Get out of the way you damn fools!' wishing earnestly that he had brought his whip with him. His anger brought very little improvement and he was left to seethe impotently as his coachman did his best, forcing the horses forward regardless of who happened to be in their path. At last, quite out of temper, Kiril descended from his carriage into the opulent entrance of the infamous Narymovna Club.

Countess Rastrelli came forward to him arms outstretched. It had been weeks since once of her most influential customers had graced the Narymovna with his presence.

'A little gambling, your Highness?' she asked, the soft lights kind to the blue-shadowed eyelids that looked crepey in the harshness of the day.

'No. I am looking for an Englishman. The Marquis of Clare. Tall, broad-shouldered, black-haired.'

Regretfully the Countess shook her head. The Englishman sounded most interesting.

'I am sorry, your Highness, only our regular clientele are gaming tonight. And not many of them. Princess Dolgorovsky's ball has claimed their attention.' She hesitated fractionally. Princess Dolgorovsky's name-day ball was one of the highlights of the social season and here was her grandson in St Petersburg's most notorious club instead of acting host at her side. It was most odd.

'Thank you, Countess,' Kiril turned to leave, wondering where best to try next. The title of Countess was purely courtesy. It was common knowledge that no Count Rastrelli had ever existed.

A doorman, resplendent in red and gold, stepped forward deferentially.

'An English gentleman answering your Highness's description arrived some minutes ago, while the Countess was attending to one of the young ladies.'

'Are you sure? Did he give his name?'

Everyone gave their name on entering the Narymovna, but it was accepted that most of them were spurious.

'Yes, your Highness. The Marquis of Clare. He demanded a bottle of champagne and is at one of the card tables and gambling for very high stakes.'

The Countess flustered. 'My apologies. If I had known . . .'

Kiril was no longer listening to her. Impatiently he waited to be divested of his cloak and gloves and strode through into the gaming room. The roulette tables were not as well attended as usual. The Countess had been right when she had complained that his grandmother's ball had robbed her of custom. At the far end of the room, behind scarlet velvet curtains, was a smaller room used for baccarat and poker. Upstairs were the mirrored and perfumed boudoirs where the Countess's gentleman clients relaxed, helped by her staff of continually changing young ladies from Paris and Moscow.

As Kiril unceremoniously entered one of the rooms it was to disturb a pillar of St Petersburg society, a flimsily clad girl on his lap, as he indulged in a game of cards with a companion he would never have acknowledged publicly. At any other time Kiril would have enjoyed the gentleman's consternation. Now he was in too much of a hurry.

He let the curtains fall behind him and undisturbed by any of the Narymovna's staff who had been given strict orders by the Countess to let the wild-eyed Prince continue his search unrestrained, he stormed into the next luxuriously-furnished vestibule.

Dominic, a full bottle of champagne in ice at his side, an empty one waiting to be disposed of on a silver tray, was deep in a hand of faro with Leon Vasileyev and waiting patiently on a couch was one of the prettiest of the Countess's new imports. With difficulty Kiril drew his eyes from unbelievably thrusting breasts beneath a gauze of chiffon, resolving to return to the Narymovna at the earliest opportunity.

'What the devil do you want?' The Marquis might have consumed a full bottle of champagne, but it didn't show in either his speech or in his eyes. Kiril wondered nervously if the Englishman carried a pistol, and remembered too late vague stories of a scandal with an outraged husband outside the Royal Box at Ascot when a pistol had been fired.

He said hurriedly, without his usual suave sophistication,

'I owe you an apology. My behaviour at Verechenko was reprehensible.'

The Marquis continued to play, ignoring the uncertainty in the eyes of his partner who desired nothing more than to leave the room.

With cool insolence the Marquis raised his eyes from the cards. 'You came within an inch of the beating of your life, Dolgorovsky,' the Marquis said as if he was speaking to a lackey. 'Unless you want it now, I advise you to leave.'

'I was under a misapprehension,' Kiril said stiffly, wishing the nubile young lady would cease posing so provocatively. Damn it all, she wasn't wearing a stitch beneath that gown. How he was expected to keep his attention on the matter in hand he didn't know.

'You are certainly under one concerning the young lady calling herself Eleanor Cartwright,' the Marquis agreed, pouring himself another glass of champagne. 'If I were you, I should find out more about her. You may be in for a shock.'

'I am well aware that Eleanor's background is a mystery,' Kiril said, trying to hold onto his temper. 'But as I am not marrying her it concerns me not in the slightest.'

The Marquis laughed mirthlessly. 'So she played for two and lost both games?'

'By God, Clare! If you continue talking about her like this, I'll plant you another one, I swear it!'

Strong muscles rippled beneath Dominic's evening jacket and he raised his eyebrows. 'I shouldn't try it if I were you.'

'I don't *want* to fight you Clare,' Kiril said exasperatedly and with truth. 'I just wish to God you would give me a chance to explain!'

'No,' Dominic said quietly. 'Let *me* explain to you.'

Without even looking at her, he motioned the young woman to leave them. Disappointedly she rose to her feet, smiling alluringly at Kiril as she disappeared through the drapes, and Leon escaped with her. Kiril dragged his attention back to Dominic.

'That young woman who wormed her way into your affections, promising to marry you at the same time as she was allowing *me* to pay court to her, is no governess and never has been.'

The conversation was not going as Kiril had intended.

'I know very well that Eleanor is more than a governess. Otherwise my grandmother would never have encouraged our marriage. That has nothing to do with my reason for seeking you out tonight.'

The Marquis shrugged. 'Maybe not. No doubt you want to tell me that you now realise she is incapable of fidelity to one man. Nevertheless I wish to tell you exactly who and what she is, and put an end to her masquerade.'

'I came,' Kiril said firmly, 'to tell you that there never *was* going to be a marriage, that . . .'

'That you already suspected,' the Marquis agreed smoothly. 'Let me set your mind at rest, my dear Prince. The young woman's background is as impeccable as her behaviour is unspeakable.'

'But I *know* that!' the Prince interrupted exasperatedly. 'Damn it, man, will you *listen* for a second?'

'I was taken in as you were.' Dominic's eyes were bruised black with pain, the lines around his mouth harsh. 'I fell in love with her years ago, when she was little more than a child. I thought her the most beautiful creature I had ever seen. She became betrothed to my brother Robert who brought her to Paris especially to show her to me. Under the circumstances we could not meet openly. My father's attitude was unbending and I was *persona non grata*. It was the only time in my life I ever envied Robert anything. When he died I was reconciled with my father. He wanted me to marry and I saw a way of marrying the only woman I had ever wanted. She wouldn't even countenance the idea. Wouldn't even meet me. Oh, I can see I was a thick-headed fool, but I knew how devoted she had been to Robert. I knew she would refuse any offer of courtship so soon after his death and so I thought that if I proposed it as a marriage of convenience, taking care of her for Robert's sake, she might accept. And, in time, learn to love me. I was a fool to think even for a moment that a girl of Catherine's spirit would marry for convenience.'

Kiril sat down slowly, listening as Dominic continued to talk as if to himself.

'I met her the night she first tried to flee. She braved the London streets alone and in the night to borrow money from a friend and some oaf assaulted her. I heard her scream and went to her assistance.' There was a long pause. 'It was very dark. I thought her a harlot and acted accordingly. Then, when I learnt from the Duchess that Catherine had fled, I left London immediately, hoping that by so doing she would feel free to return. On board the *Gretel*, despite her attempts to disguise her appearance, I recognised her, not only as the young woman I had treated so freely, but as Catherine Davencourt, the girl my brother had loved and wanted to marry. The girl I had loved at a distance for years.'

'But then why didn't you tell her you knew her real identity?'

'Because I am a fool,' Dominic said savagely, slamming his fist onto the table. 'It was pleasurable teasing her, allowing her to think I thought her a reformed harlot. And I wanted to make her want me as I wanted her. She would have nothing to do with me for weeks, but then, the day war was declared, I knew she felt the same as I did.' He ran a hand despairingly through his thick hair. 'I was going to tell her this evening that I knew all along who she was, and then you burst in and I realised what a fool I had been. I had been taken in by her beauty, by Robert's description of her sweetness and vitality. Thank God he never knew what a faithless whore she is at heart. To allow me to kiss her, desire her as I did and to respond to it. And all the time to intend marrying you to become a Princess!'

The dark eyes blazed with torment. 'I wasted years of my life on a dream woman that didn't exist. A pretty mirage without substance. Well, I'll waste no more! She can rot in hell now. I'll never see her again,' and he strode backwards and forwards across the red plush room a nerve twitching at the corner of the white-lipped mouth.

'But she loves you!' Kiril protested.

'No doubt she told you she loved you as well, otherwise you would never have asked her to marry you!'

'But she didn't! She said she would think about it and
that was only because I told her that you were to marry
Amelia Cunningham.'

Dominic stopped his marching and in one quick movement pinned Kiril against the wall. 'I never proposed
marriage to that sly-eyed cat, and well you know it!'

'You paid her enough attention,' Kiril protested,
hoping that the Marquis had not damaged the expensive
lace of his shirt front.

'To make Catherine jealous,' he hissed, as if talking to
a child. 'Do you know nothing of how a woman's mind
works?'

Kiril felt he did but that now was not the time to say so.
He remained silent.

'So she never *did* say she would marry you?' Dominic
showed no intention of releasing Kiril, he held him by
the throat his eyes burning into his.

'No. Tonight she told me she loved you. That she
could never love another man. She was half out of her
mind with grief.'

Dominic let go of him so suddenly Kiril stumbled.

'Where are you going?' he asked, picking himself to
his feet as Dominc wrenched the curtains to one side.

'Where am I going?' Dominic said. 'To Catherine of
course!' And the curtains swished behind him, leaving
Kiril breathless and dazed as he struggled to adjust his
shirt frills to their usual perfection.

CHAPTER
TEN

AMELIA had been well aware of Dominic's absence from the ballroom. One waltz with her and he had disappeared—and so had that red-haired creature.

As she circled the polished floor in the arms of an elderly Arch-Duke she caught sight of her mother's face and froze inwardly. Lady Cunningham was obviously in the grip of barely-controlled passion. The dance seemed endless. Not waiting to hear the Arch-Duke's thanks as the music finally finished playing, she made her way hastily to her mother's side. 'What is it? What is the matter, Mama?'

'Not here.' Lady Cunningham clicked her fan shut, forcing a smile across at Countess Nestoreva who was watching her. 'Take a glass of champagne and we will seek some air on the balcony.' Her voice was trembling with suppressed emotion.

Hardly able to contain her impatience, Amelia took a glass of champagne and strolled with apparent nonchalance onto the flower-decked balcony with its myriad fairylights.

Lady Cunningham carefully avoided the couples who were also seeking seclusion. At last, satisfied she would not be overheard, she said grimly, 'Princess Dagmar's companion coerced the Marquis into one of the smaller salons, a *darkened* salon!'

Amelia drew in a swift intake of breath, her lips tightening.

'Fortunately the children's nanny saw them and had the sense to inform the Prince. Of course the Princess is saying that the Marquis forced his attentions on her companion and that the girl called for help, but *I* know which version to believe.'

'And what happened—was happening—when the Prince entered the salon?' Amelia's fingers curved, itching to scratch long weals down Catherine's cheeks.

Lady Cunningham wasn't sure whether it was best to tell her daughter or not. She still hoped to gain the Marquis for a son-in-law and men would always be men. A pretty face and a willing one and they all behaved like fools. She had the good sense to realise that the Marquis had entered that candle-lit salon of his own free will, but it would not do to give her daughter that impression.

'The hussy was forcing herself upon him, wrapping her arms round his neck. The whole affair was perfectly disgusting. Naturally the Marquis was trying to disentangle himself. But the Prince was so mad with rage— apparently he *was* going to marry her—that he would not listen to reason. The Marquis told him what a harlot the girl was and the Prince knocked him to the ground.'

'Harlot?' Amelia's eyes, so soft and appealing by day, and hard by night, lit up. 'Did he actually call her a harlot?'

'Oh yes!' Lady Cunningham's informant had been most insistent on that point and it gave her Ladyship great satisfaction. 'But the damage is done, Amelia. The Marquis has left Verechenko and without proposing to you.'

'And all because of that common-place little slut!' In a vengeful fury she swept back into the ballroom, disregarding her mother's restraining hand.

There was no sign of the sea-green satin and lovely head of red-gold hair crowned by a single perfect rose. Instinct led Amelia from the ballroom to the private apartments upstairs. She stopped a footman, enquiring as to the whereabouts of the suite of rooms occupied by Princess Dagmar's companion. Obediently the footman led the way. As they stopped outside an exquisitely carved door, Amelia dismissed him curtly. Then, without even the courtesy of knocking, she flung the door open and entered. Vilya rushed forward protestingly, then, seeing who the invader was, fell back uncertainly. Catherine raised a tear-stained face from her arms, staring in bewilderment.

Even with eyes red-rimmed from crying and cheeks scored by tears, Catherine's beauty was undeniable. Amelia glared at her in hatred.

'He's gone! Because of you he's gone!'

A vicious hand slapped Catherine's cheek, nearly knocking her off the satin-padded stool. 'You weren't satisfied with Kiril were you? You had to have him as well!' She laughed mirthlessly. 'He's not such a fool as the Prince. He knows what you are. A harlot. That's what he called you, isn't it? A harlot. And the Prince knows now too. You'll never be Princess Dolgorova now. But I shall be Marchioness of Clare. I am going to him at the Nestorevs' to tell him I realise the scene was none of his fault. That you flaunted yourself, compromised him. I shan't lose him because of a gutter-snipe like you!' And she slammed the door behind her leaving

Vilya open-mouthed in amazement.

The Nestorevs'. He'd gone to the Nestorevs'. Of course, that was where he would go. They were the only other Russian family he was on intimate terms with. Whether he would marry Amelia, Catherine had no way of knowing. She only knew that whatever he did, she couldn't bear to go on living if he thought that the magical ecstasy of their brief afternoon together, and their few precious, fateful moments in the salon, had meant nothing more to her than a light flirtation. He had to know that she had never promised herself to Kiril. That her feelings for him reached to the very depth of her being. If he still wanted nothing further to do with her, then she would have to accept it. But to allow him to continue thinking her nothing but a flirt and a tease was unbearable.

'My gown and coat,' she said to Vilya, rising shakily to her feet.

'But Miss Eleanor . . .'

'My gown and coat, Vilya.' Not even bothering to slip her arms into the sleeves she flung the sable around her shoulders and low-cut dress and ran from the room.

The music from the ballroom filled the palace, couples, arm in arm, gazed strangely at her as she hurried down the main staircase. She had to get a carriage or the Panhard. But the chauffeur had been given the evening off and the grounds were so crammed with the carriages of guests that she didn't know where to start looking for the one bearing either the Vishnetski or Dolgorovsky emblems.

'You seem distressed. May I be of assistance?'

She turned to meet the expressionless eyes of Captain

Bestuzhev. Catherine forgot her instinctive dislike of him. 'I need a carriage. Urgently.'

Bestuzhev's bald head shone beneath the glittering lights. 'Allow me to offer you mine.'

'Oh thank you!'

Bestuzhev wiped his bull-like neck with a large hand-kerchief and followed Catherine outside, the evening was proving more interesting than even he could have hoped for.

Seconds later Captain Bestuzhev's carriage was rolling to a halt and Bestuzhev was offering her his hand.

'I am most grateful, Captain.'

'Am I allowed to ask where it is you are going in such a desperate hurry, Mademoiselle?'

'To the Nestorevs'.'

'But the Count and Countess are here, at the ball.'

'I know. It is someone else I have to see. Thank you for your help.'

Catherine was impatient to say goodbye, for the coachman to whip the horses to a gallop.

'I cannot allow you to travel unattended, Made-moiselle,' Bestuzhev said, entering the carriage and closing the door behind him. He knocked on the wall and the coachman flicked the reins, the horses beginning to trot away from Verechenko.

Catherine was slightly flustered. She had not antici-pated him joining her, but she was too concerned with reaching Dominic in the shortest possible time for it to cause her unnecessary alarm.

'You slipped away from me the last time we were together,' Bestuzhev said, and in the dim light of the coach she could see his thick lips parting in a smile.

'The party was too boisterous for my liking,' she said, remembering all too clearly how she had made a hasty exit from the circle of the whirling dancers and how Dominic had kissed her on the darkened terrace steps, confirming what she had known in her heart since their first, brief meeting. Tonight would probably be their last one. It was a thought too painful to be borne. She clenched her hands together, struggling to hold back the tears.

'But tonight is not boisterous,' Bestuzhev leaned back, completely at his ease, feeling the sweat break out on the palms of his fleshy hands. Catherine wished he would cease to make small talk.

They were crossing the Neva now, the water shining jet black beneath them.

'And this is a perfect setting for two people to become better acquainted.'

Catherine's thoughts were elsewhere. The streets and squares looked different at night. She struggled to remember the way to the Nestorevs' and was certain that they were going in the wrong direction. She saw the lights of the opera house and her suspicions were confirmed.

'Your coachman is lost. This is not the way to the Nestorevs'.'

Bestuzhev laughed, the powerful thigh muscles showing beneath his breeches as he crossed his legs negligently.

'Indeed it is not. Your errand can wait a little longer. After we have enjoyed what you are so obviously seeking.'

Catherine stared at him uncomprehendingly. 'But I

must go to the Nestorevs' at once! You are taking great liberties with me in not doing as I ask.'

Bestuzhev's fat lips parted and he reached across the carriage, his sweating hand enclosing Catherine's slender wrist.

'That is nothing to the liberties I am about to take, Mademoiselle.'

With sickening clarity Catherine realised his intentions and her predicament.

'You have made a mistake,' she whispered hoarsely. 'I am not that sort of a woman. You must return me to Verechenko immediately.'

The grip on her wrist increased so that it was all she could do not to cry out in pain.

'That is not what I have heard, Mademoiselle. I believe you are going to the Nestorevs' in order to be *very* accommodating to a certain young gentleman. But first we will visit my apartment. Some champagne and brandy will soon overcome your shyness.'

Catherine's initial shock was over. Her eyes glinted dangerously. 'I shall scream.'

'Scream as much as you like. My coachman will take not the slightest notice. In fact he is quite accustomed to such protests.'

With her free hand, Catherine clutched her fur to her throat, concealing the low décolletage of her dress. Bestuzhev, seeing the movement, laughed. He was in no hurry and a fight only made the final conquest all the sweeter. The hoof-beats changed tempo. The carriage was slowing down. The street outside was dark and empty.

Catherine contemplated kicking him hard and then

running as far as she could. She was given no opportunity. With a quick, practised movement, Bestuzhev had grabbed her other wrist and now held them tightly behind her back as the coachman, eyes blank, opened the carriage door and Bestuzhev proceeded to push a vainly struggling Catherine across a small stretch of pavement, up a narrow flight of unlit stairs and into an ornate room.

As he released the hold of one hand in turning the key in the lock behind him, Catherine swung round, her nails scoring deep scratchmarks down his cheek. His only reaction was one of pleasure. It had been a long time since he had enjoyed a fight with such a beautiful wild-cat. He released her other wrist and as she ran from him, searching for other doors, other exits, he slowly and purposefully divested himself of his jacket and shirt.

There were no other doors. No servants. No people in the street below to hear her cries. Frantically Catherine turned to see Bestuzhev moving towards her, naked to the waist, wet lips parted in lust.

'What do you mean you don't know where she is?' Dominic resisted an overwhelming urge to shake Baroness Kerenskaya till the rosebuds fell from her hair.

'The Princess has been searching for her this last half hour. No-one has seen her.'

Dominic took the stairs two at a time, oblivious of the interest he was causing. He hammered on the door of Catherine's room so loudly that Vilya, who had had enough excitement for one day, thought she would faint in fear.

Nervously she opened it the merest fraction, only to

have it pushed wide as Dominic strode in, looking around him like a man demented.

'Where is she? Where is Catherine?'

Vilya had no idea who Catherine was and wondered if the Marquis was mad.

'I don't know anyone by that name, my Lord. Perhaps if you ask the footman. There are so many guests and . . .'

'Your mistress!' Dominic shouted at her, unable to control his patience any longer. 'Where is she?'

'She has gone, my Lord.'

'Gone?' Dominic stopped short. 'Gone where?'

Vilya was completely out of her depth. 'After the quarrel with the other English lady she asked for her coat and ran from the room. I have no idea where she has gone.'

Dominic realised he was terrifying the maid half to death and that he would get no sense out of her if he did so. He struggled for control.

'What quarrel? What was said?'

Knowing that the quarrel had been about the very gentleman who stood towering above her, his eyes flashing beneath black brows like the devil incarnate, Vilya was at a loss.

'Come on girl. I won't eat you! What was said? I must find her, can't you understand?'

Vilya couldn't, but was unable to hold out any longer.

'The English girl, the blonde one, said she wasn't going to lose you over a—a gutter-snipe I think was the expression, my Lord. She said she was going immediately to the Nestorevs' and she slapped Miss Eleanor across the face and swept out of the room like a tornado.'

'And then?' Dominic would reckon with Amelia Cunningham later.

'And then Miss Eleanor asked for her coat and ran from the room without another word.'

Dominic was already at the door. The Nestorevs', she had gone to the Nestorevs'.

He raced back down the stairs, ignoring the protests of the distinguished guests he was thrusting aside, and sent a servant for a carriage.

As the Vishnetskis' coachman cantered the horses to Verechenko's entrance, Dominic said to the waiting doorman: 'How long since the Princess's companion left in the Dolgorovskys' carriage?'

'The young lady left, but not in the Dolgorovsky carriage. Captain Bestuzhev escorted her.'

Dominic froze. 'Bestuzhev?'

'Yes, your Lordship. The young lady was distressed and the Captain offered her the use of his carriage.'

Dominic knew Bestuzhev. His throat tightened. The thought of Catherine alone in a carriage with that lecherous monster appalled him. He ordered the coachman to whip the horses to a frenzy and tried to persuade himself that Bestuzhev would act honourably as the carriage threaded its way through St Petersburg to the Nestorevs' imposing residence.

Only a few lights were on. The Count and Countess were at the Princess's ball. Only the servants remained, ready to carry out any whim their master and mistress might request when they returned.

'Count Bestuzhev arrived with Princess Dagmar's companion only a short while ago. Please conduct me to them at once.'

The footman shook his powdered head. 'Lady Cunningham and her daughter are in the salon awaiting your presence, your Lordship. But there have been no other visitors.'

The Vishnetski coach had driven like a bat out of hell, but it would still have been impossible to overtake the Captain's carriage with the start he had had.

'Shall I tell her Ladyship you have arrived?'

'No.' The Marquis swung on his heel. Lady Cunningham and Amelia could wait there all night for all he cared. Where was Catherine and Bestuzhev? That Bestuzhev had seen an opportunity of taking advantage of Catherine, Dominic did not doubt for a moment. Where would he have taken her? Even a girl as spirited as Catherine could offer no defence against an ox of a man like Bestuzhev. With every passing second Bestuzhev would be forcing his attentions on her, taking that slender body with brutal force.

'Bestuzhev?' Dominic said harshly to the coachman. 'Do you know where he lives?'

'He quarters with the Regiment, but he has a private apartment in the city.'

'Then take me there,' Dominic pressed a fistful of roubles into his hand. 'Force the horses to the limit, understand?'

The coachman understood. While Dominic suffered torments, imagining Catherine's body broken and bruised in Bestuzhev's arms, the coachman lashed the horses to a frenzy, pounding over the bridge and through the wide squares to the smaller streets and the Captain's apartment.

Dominic did not wait for the carriage to halt. Dementedly he raced up the narrow staircase, wrestling with the doorknob, hammering his fists on the door, shouting. 'Catherine! Catherine!'

There was an answering cry and Dominic yelled for the coachman as he threw his whole might against the door.

The coachman, who hadn't seen so much drama since Prince Charykov had shot Count Danileck, joined in with gusto.

The wood split, the hinges gave and the two men hurled themselves into the room.

As the door began to give way, Bestuzhev had rolled his weight off Catherine, stumbling wildly across the room for his jacket and his pistol. Dominic had a glimpse of Catherine, her gown torn to the waist, her breasts bare, her hair cascading over her shoulders, and then he saw the glint of metal and Bestuzhev's hands closed on the pistol. Catherine screamed, Dominic dived, his hands closing around Bestuzhev's, as Bestuzhev struggled to lift the pistol into a firing position.

The coachman grabbed at Bestuzhev's legs, knocking him off balance, and Catherine, careless of her nakedness flew across the room, biting and kicking Bestuzhev so that with a cry of agony he fell and the pistol dropped on the floor.

'Don't, sir! Don't shoot him!' the coachman implored. 'It would cause a terrible scandal. The young lady . . .' He kept his back to Catherine and tried to behave as he felt a gentleman should.

Bestuzhev cowered and blustered. Dominic stood, legs parted, the pistol pointing at Bestuzhev's head, and Catherine clung to his arm.

'No, my love! No! It's all right, you came in time. It's all right!'

Restraining himself from pulling the trigger was the hardest thing Dominic, Marquis of Clare, had ever done. Slowly he lowered the pistol and handed it to the relieved coachman.

Then he turned to Catherine, seeing with agony the purple bruises already colouring her neck and breasts. Gently he lifted the torn remnants of her dress to cover the rose-red nipples.

'Forgive me, Catherine,' he said huskily.

'There is nothing to forgive, my love.'

The beaten Bestuzhev watched sullenly, the coachman pleasurably as Dominic took Catherine into his arms and kissed her long and deeply.

As he withdrew his head from hers she said, wonderingly,

'You called me Catherine. When did you know?'

With ease he picked her up in his arms, the fury spent, the amusement that she always aroused in him returning.

'I have always known. I have always loved you.'

Gently he carried her down the stairs and into the Vishnetski carriage. She nestled against him, as his lips brushed her hair, her cheeks.

'I fell in love with you years ago, even before you were engaged to Robert.'

'But how could you have?' she protested, gazing up at him in joy. 'We'd never met.'

'No,' he agreed, pulling her so close to him that their hearts seemed to beat as one. 'But I used to visit London incognito to see Robert. I saw you then, but was in no position to court you. And you become engaged to Robert. And he brought you to Paris and I saw you again and again and everything he told me about you only made me love you more.'

Robert. The name hung between them.

'I loved him very much,' Catherine said softly, 'and I would have been very happy with him. But the love Robert and I shared was not like this. It was gentle and tender and I was content with it.'

'Both of us loved Robert,' Dominic said gently. 'And Robert, above all people would be happy for us, and would understand.'

'Yes.' She lifted her mouth once more to his.

With Dominic she would find all Robert's gentleness and tenderness, and something else. Something that made her spine shiver and her flesh melt. Something so powerful it united the two of them against the world. They had arrived at the brilliantly lit entrance of Verechenko, but neither Dominic nor Catherine were even vaguely aware of it.